He took the tip of her finger in his mouth and bit it gently.

Sensation scorched through her, kindling a needfire so violent it burned away the last rational promptings of her brain. If only she'd had some experience—but even that thought died, for Hope was glad she had never felt like this before, never wanted this. Only Keir—and Keir was all her world....

"You're wet," she said, her voice husky. "Take off your shirt and I'll put it in the dryer."

"You take it off," he said, his narrowed eyes gleaming. He stepped back and held out his arms, challenging her in the most stark, basic way of all—the primitive sexual challenge of man to woman.

Take what you want, his tone, his expression said.

If you dare...

ROBYN DONALD has always lived in Northland in New Zealand, initially on her father's stud dairy farm in Warkworth, then in the Bay of Islands, an area of great natural beauty, where she lives today with her husband and an ebullient and mostly Labrador dog. She resigned from her teaching position when she found she enjoyed writing romances more, and now spends any time not writing in reading, gardening, traveling and writing letters to keep up with her two adult children and her friends.

Books by Robyn Donald

HARLEQUIN PRESENTS®
1980—THE NANNY AFFAIR
2012—A FORBIDDEN DESIRE
2108—FORBIDDEN PLEASURE
2162—A RELUCTANT MISTRESS

Don't miss any of our special offers. Write to us at the following address for information on our newest releases.

Harlequin Reader Service
U.S.: 3010 Walden Ave., P.O. Box 1325, Buffalo, NY 14269
Canadian: P.O. Box 609, Fort Erie, Ont. L2A 5X3

Robyn Donald
THE DEVIL'S BARGAIN

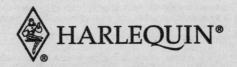

TORONTO • NEW YORK • LONDON
AMSTERDAM • PARIS • SYDNEY • HAMBURG
STOCKHOLM • ATHENS • TOKYO • MILAN • MADRID
PRAGUE • WARSAW • BUDAPEST • AUCKLAND

ISBN 0-373-12246-2

THE DEVIL'S BARGAIN

First North American Publication 2002.

Copyright © 2001 by Robyn Donald.

PROLOGUE

SHE huddled out on the tiny ornamental balcony, unable to move, unable to force the hands covering her face to block her ears. Darkness and the chill of an autumn evening in New Zealand pressed onto her, but the slow shivers that shook her slender body came from her heart.

Echoes of her father's words tumbled around her head, monstrous, shameful. 'Come to some agreement with me and you can have Hope,' he'd said, as though his daughter were a stock option. 'Try a hostile takeover, and you can say good-bye to any chance with her.' His voice had altered. 'If I forbid her to go out with you, she'll obey. You can bet money on that.'

Humiliation swept over the listener in disgusting waves as she waited for Keir's scornful response.

But when his voice came it was almost amused. 'What makes you think I want to marry Hope? I can see the advantage for you, but what's in it for me?'

Hope moaned silently as her father gave a disbelieving laugh. 'Come on, Carmichael, you want her—you've been escorting her for the past two months. Men of your stamp don't sleep with kids—your other women have known what they were doing, whereas Hope's a complete innocent. So it's got to be marriage. Makes sense—she'd be a good, docile wife, and she knows everyone who's anyone in New Zealand. And she gets everything when I die.'

There was a long silence. Tension screwed through Hope, tightening into pain as she held her breath.

Eventually Keir said in a reflective voice, 'All right, let's deal.'

Hope's heart missed a couple of beats; desperately she longed for it stop so she could die. But it began again, relentlessly forcing her to participate in the degradation of all her fragile, precious hopes.

Her father said heartily, 'Marry her, and you'll get the firm without this undignified fight for it. I'll sign it over to you legally; all I want is to run it until I'm ready to retire.' He paused significantly, before continuing in deliberately weighted words, 'Otherwise you're going to have a fight on your hands. I know a lot of tricks and some very important people; if I have to, I'll drag your little merchant bank down into the gutter.'

Locked in a nightmare, Hope pressed her closed fist against her mouth, forcing back the choked agony that lodged there.

Perhaps it *was* a nightmare—perhaps she was dreaming this...

Keir's icy, contemptuous voice shattered that illusion. 'Offering a daughter as a sacrifice to stave off ruin died out a couple of hundred years ago. Why would I want an eighteen-year-old wife? Try all your tricks, call up as many debts and favours as you can, but I'll take over your business one way or another.'

There was a charged silence.

'All right,' her father said sullenly, 'forget marriage. You want her—take her, then. She's pretty enough, God knows, to keep you happy until you get tired of her.'

'You want to sell her to me?' Keir sounded coolly incredulous—but not, the listener realised with a despairing sob, either surprised or disgusted. 'You must be desperate. Apart from anything else, she might have other ideas.'

A note she recognised hardened her father's voice as he said, 'She'll do as she's told.'

'You know the trick?' Keir sounded amused.

Frozen, sick to her soul, Hope felt her heart crack as she

waited for the man she loved to reject her father's obscene offer.

'I know the trick,' James Sanderson said, something like a gloating pleasure showing through his tone.

'She's pretty and sweet and charming enough,' Keir agreed thoughtfully. 'Unfortunately I don't have time to teach an innocent all the things a woman needs to know to keep a man satisfied. I expect my money's worth from the women I support, and Hope doesn't know the first thing about sensuality. Besides, as you say, she's besotted. I could have had her any time this last month, just by snapping my fingers.'

Another long silence. Then her father said in a low, furious voice, 'I see. You've been playing a double game all along—trotting her out so that you can pump her about me.'

'Why else would I take out a child straight from school? Not that she was particularly profitable—she doesn't know anything about your business.' His voice changed into hard ruthlessness. 'Accept it, Sanderson, you're in an untenable position. Your business is going down the drain because you're a greedy fool who hasn't bothered to adapt over the past forty years. If you want to deal, make it something that works for me as well as you. Otherwise you're wasting my time.'

At long last Hope managed to wrench her hands up to cover her ears, to block out betrayal. Through the roaring in her head she heard her heart break.

CHAPTER ONE

'Thank you, madam.' Hope waited until the customer began to sign the credit card slip before letting her amber-gold gaze drift furtively the length of the shop to the man waiting inside the door—if waiting it could be called when his impatience iced the interior of the glitzy shop.

It *was* Keir Carmichael.

Blinking, Hope jerked her attention back to the counter, but in spite of herself she sneaked another glance at Keir, now frowning at an ornate diamond necklace that made up in tastelessness what it lacked in beauty.

Outside in the bright Australian sunlight people in holiday mood called out and waved, their voices lifting into laughter—an ironic background to the panic that kicked her in the stomach. In spite of clothes crafted for him by a master tailor there was nothing elegantly refined about Keir. Six foot three of broad-shouldered, long-legged, lean-hipped masculinity, he projected raw, uncompromising dominance.

'There you are.' The customer's patrician accent didn't hide her impatience, or the trace of New Zealand beneath the vowels.

'Thank you.' Forcing the words past her constricted throat, Hope pushed the platinum credit card back across the counter.

Slender, pampered fingers picked it up and stowed it into an expensive leather billfold which was then slid into a Prada bag. No rings, Hope noted compulsively. So the woman who'd bought the clever goanna clip, its sinuous lines perfect for a lapel or a scarf, wasn't married to—anyone.

8

Matching Hope's smile, the woman took the small parcel and turned towards the door. When she reached Keir she said in a voice just loud enough for Hope to hear, 'There, that didn't take long, did it?'

The man she'd kept waiting gave her a cool, considering look. Hope controlled the curl of her lip, but perhaps he sensed her scorn because he lifted his head abruptly and flicked a glance her way.

It was like being lashed by hailstones. Although Keir Carmichael was dark—sable hair, black brows and lashes, olive skin—his eyes blazed the frigid, colourless grey of the sky on a frosty dawn; they swept her face with a biting indifference that ached right down to her bones.

He really didn't recognise her. Instead of overpowering relief she felt shattered, hollowed out by tension and a bitter, furious disappointment.

Killing her first response—a glare—Hope set her lips into a stiff little smile. One of Keir's dark brows lifted in a movement as insulting as it was deliberate before he turned and walked out the door, the woman clinging happily to his arm.

Hope's breath hissed through her teeth. You don't have to run from him ever again, she told herself, trying to rein in her crazy pulse by putting away the exquisitely made pins, each one worth more than she'd earn in a month. Her long fingers shook as she replaced the gold koala with smoky Argyle diamonds for eyes, a sterling silver cluster of gumnuts, a spray of wildflowers in the subtly hued sapphires of southern Queensland—frivolous, costly toys a rich man might buy his mistress or wife as a souvenir.

Keir Carmichael turning up on the morning of her twenty-third birthday—oh, what a dirty, cynical little trick for fate to play! Yet Hope was humiliatingly glad she'd worn a creamy silk blouse that set off her skin, and a black skirt short enough to reveal excellent legs.

'Ah...miss?' Sweating slightly, a young man accosted her

with a tentative smile, his blond hair tangled around deeply tanned shoulders. Eyeing her with an assumed cockiness that didn't hide his lack of confidence, he visibly relaxed in the warmth of her smile. 'That necklace in the window—the pearl beads—how much are they?'

'They're not beads,' Hope warned him gently. 'I'm afraid they're the real thing.' She told him the price.

Blenching, he muttered, 'Out of my range. Thank you.'

Outside in the street a girl stared at the pearls, sun-bleached hair almost hiding her yearning eyes.

Hope said, 'Would your friend like to try them on?'

'I can't afford them,' he said, backing away.

Hope grinned. 'So? Memories don't have to cost anything.'

He frowned, then gave a quick nod and loped through the doors into the blazing sunlight. As the girl looked up eagerly Hope felt an odd little catch of pain. Had she ever been that young? Never, not even as a child.

Chloe, the other shop assistant, commented in a low voice, 'Those kids can't even afford the dust on the floor here.'

'She'll always remember what she looked like in them.' Hope took the cabinet key from beneath the counter. 'And one day she might become a tycoon and make a sentimental pilgrimage here to buy some.'

'She's not tycoon material if she goes around with surfies,' Chloe responded with sour pessimism.

The two youngsters came in and Hope went over to unlock the window case. With the shimmering rope of moonlight in her hands she turned—and met the frozen glance of the man who had so comprehensively snubbed her only a few minutes previously.

Except that now the aloof indifference in his eyes had been replaced by speculation.

Terror stabbed through her—stupid, baseless terror, because she was no longer a foolish, romantic adolescent drowning in the throes of her first love affair.

Pinning her rescued smile more tightly to her lips, she took the pearls to the counter. Over the shuddering tattoo of her heartbeats she murmured, 'Here you are,' and laid the pearls onto a pad of black velvet. 'They're called Broome blues because they come from Broome in Western Australia and they have a faint bluish sheen. Let's see how they look on you.'

Five endless minutes later, after the girl had gazed at her reflection with a solemn, almost bewildered awe, the two kids smiled at Hope and said together, 'Thanks a lot.' Laughing at each other, they linked little fingers and walked out of the shop and into the sunlight outside, young, carefree, confidently in love—enviable.

'Could you bring those here, please?' Chloe's abrupt request forced Hope to turn.

Stiff-backed, her expression rigidly controlled, she walked across the shop floor with the heavy, warm pearls in her hand. Keir watched her with hooded, unreadable eyes, no recognition relaxing his hard, authoritative face or softening the mouth that had once possessed hers in a dark, mindless enchantment.

'Mr Carmichael would like to see the pearl string,' Chloe said, looking from one to the other. 'Perhaps you could show him?'

With elaborate care Hope set the necklace down. Crisply, keeping her eyes on the pearls, she said, 'They're a matched string, sir. They've taken over ten years to find, and—'

'I'd like to see them on,' he interrupted.

Four years ago he'd been twenty-six, and well aware of the impact of his low, textured voice, its confidence emphasised by a thread of sensuality that charged it with untamed danger, like the glimpse of a wolf in an arctic landscape. Now that potent male sexuality was underpinned by an authority as relentless as a blizzard.

The harshly angular framework of his face proclaimed a man in complete control of himself and the kingdom he'd carved out, a man whose ruthlessness made him feared as well as respected.

'On?' The word splintered in Hope's mouth.

'Yes.' Keir flicked another of those icy glances at Chloe, waiting until she moved discreetly away before transferring his crystalline gaze back to Hope. 'Put them on.'

Everything in her rose up in outraged rebellion at the unemphatic command. For a furiously reckless moment she toyed with the idea of flinging the pearls at him and telling him to try them on himself; fortunately, common sense shrieked a warning.

When she'd been three she'd climbed up on the kitchen steps, opened the lid of the deep freeze and reached into its forbidden depths; discovering her there, her father had deliberately pressed her small, starfish hand against the side, holding it in place until ice burned the skin.

The same powerlessness and bewilderment and outrage imprisoned her now. Dry-mouthed, as shamed as though she'd been ordered to strip, she picked up the string with shaky hands and ignored the catch to drop them over her head. Her breath locked in her lungs as she met his eyes with a steady, stony stare.

In an indifferent tone Keir said, 'They're the wrong shade. You need pearls with a touch of warmth to go with that skin and hair.'

A terrifying sensual heat—relic of the time when the slightest look from this man had stirred her body to turmoil—warred with anger and pride. Returning the string to the velvet pad, she said curtly, 'Pearls need to be tried on by the woman you plan to buy them for.'

'Thank you,' he said, and added, 'Hope.'

Her heart gave an enormous thump. After a shocked second she lifted her lashes and strove for an ironic note, settling instead for deadpan calmness. 'You always were good at mind games, Keir, but what was the purpose of this one?'

'You pretended not to recognise me.'

He waited with devastating courtesy while she discarded meaningless responses. After a moment that stretched tautly into discomfort, he finished, 'So who was playing the game, Hope?'

His gaze moved with leisurely thoroughness across her face, took in the long, slender line of her throat and the swell of her breasts below the cream silk.

It was a purely male assessment, appreciative and primally charged. To her intense chagrin Hope's body responded with a wild urgency so that she had to stiffen her disintegrating spine as her fingers clenched onto the black velvet pad.

Jerking her hands from the counter, she hid them behind her. 'I thought you might not want to be recognised,' she said, hoping she sounded worldly and sophisticated. She added, 'You might be on a—*private*—holiday.'

A smile—equivocal, enigmatic—lifted the corners of his mouth. 'You can do better than that. Why wouldn't I want to be recognised by a beautiful woman?'

Hope sent desperate thought-waves at the other assistant, but with studious detachment Chloe went on tidying gold chains.

Outside people and cars eased down the narrow street and a warm wind rustled the palms. Inside it was so quiet Hope could hear the blood quicken through her body, the taut urgency of instinct warning her to get out of there.

Keir said, 'You've changed, of course. That rather touching childish fairness has mellowed into a sunlit beauty—your hair's the smoky, dusky gold of manuka honey, almost the same colour as your eyes.' Once more he subjected her to a slow, sensually loaded scrutiny, and once more her body hummed in blind, mindless, humiliating response.

'You've changed, too,' she said crisply.

His smile dismissed this. 'Four years ago you were lovely, Hope, but now you glow. Even your skin is like pale honey-coloured silk. Perhaps it's the Australian sun. Or is it a man?'

The question—delivered without inflection—slid so smoothly through her defences that she answered without thinking, 'No.' No men, ever; somehow Keir had killed the normal responses in her, imprinted her so that she froze when any other man touched her.

Perhaps because she'd been so young when she'd fallen in love—perhaps because that love had been cruelly betrayed—she'd been programmed to find only arrogantly angular features sexy, to thrill only when ice-coloured eyes met hers, to want only a tall man with broad shoulders and long legs and an effortless, formidable air of command.

'Do you plan to live in Noosa permanently?'

'As long as I work here.' Did the cool, almost amused tone successfully disguise her churning emotions? 'I assume you *are* on holiday?'

'For a week. We must get together and catch up on the past four years.' Ice-clear eyes examined her face with the keen concentration of a diamond cutter about to tap a stone worth a million dollars.

Hope's heart lurched, missed several beats, then struggled into an uneven canter. Why, oh, why hadn't she chosen to work in a busy café? Here, in this calm, quiet shop, she was a sitting duck. Chloe wasn't going to come near her, and even if her boss looked in he'd assume she was selling the pearls and leave her to it.

Keir Carmichael might wield a powerful sexuality that still had the power to reduce her to witlessness—might be the only man who could break through to her guarded femininity—but he was a treacherous swine who'd carelessly smashed her life.

With a smile that showed her teeth, she said, 'I don't think that would be a good idea.'

'Why?'

Keeping the smile pinned on, she said, 'Because we have nothing in common. We never did.' Except her father's firm.

'You didn't think that four years ago,' Keir said evenly, his heavy lids and thick lashes almost hiding his eyes.

Words she'd heard him say to her father rang in her ears. The intervening years hadn't diluted their poisonous impact, nor her humiliation.

Anger fired her eyes to gems, prickled across her skin. In a voice as smooth as the honey he'd compared her hair to, she said, 'Ah, but I was so naïve and easily influenced four years ago.'

His lashes drooped further. His face was sculpted into the fierce beauty of a predator, all angles and tough, disciplined patience. 'Naïve, perhaps, but I wouldn't have called you easily influenced. You were intelligent and passionate and funny, with a maturity that made you seem older than your age. But you're right—this is no place to be talking about the past. When do you get off for lunch?'

Why not? They could exchange platitudes and she had the perfect excuse to leave early. And it would get him off her back. If Keir had made up his mind to see her she might as well go along with him. He hadn't got to where he was by giving up.

But it would be surrender. Although she might not be able to control her response to him, she could certainly deny him that small victory.

'If you're asking me to lunch,' she said lightly, 'the answer is no, thank you.' To show that she wasn't afraid she gave him her most charming smile. 'It's been interesting to see you again, but that part of my life is long past and I've always felt that raking over old embers is one of the more unprofitable things anyone can do.' She allowed a touch of malice to shade her voice. 'And profit is so important, isn't it?'

Eyes glittering like diamond shards, he reduced to mere stage scenery the marble floor, the shiny glass cases where skilfully crafted baubles reflected light in a radiance of colours, the sophisticated, carefully composed holiday ambience of the best jewellery salon in one of Australia's premier resorts.

'Not as important as friends, surely?' he drawled.

His words rubbed an old wound. Deliberately relaxing her clenched jaw, Hope said, 'If you don't want to buy anything I'm afraid I must ask you to go. My boss doesn't encourage personal visits.'

Turning sideways, she groped for the keys to the window cabinet, straightened with them in her hand, and reached for the necklace. Keir's hand came down over hers, imprisoning it against the smooth, warm roundness of the pearls, the tactile opulence of the velvet pad.

His touch roared through her with all the subtlety and gentleness of an express train, smashing barriers, shattering four years of effort and self-discipline in one crazy second. White-faced, she said in a tone so low the words barely made it past her lips, 'Let me go.'

He lifted his hand, and her treacherous, unreliable, decadent body ached helplessly.

Keir's voice was a threatening, fascinating mixture of mockery and powerful sexuality. 'Who are you afraid of, Hope? Me or yourself?'

Arrogant bastard! Did he think she'd be a push-over? And why the devil did he want to see her again? There had to be a reason—Keir Carmichael always had a reason for every action.

Biting back hot, reckless words, Hope said in her most

politely colourless voice, 'Neither.' She waited before adding delicately, 'Your...companion...might not like being neglected.'

'Aline is an employee,' he said, narrowed silver eyes scanning her face, 'and, for the record, when I'm with one woman I don't ask another out.'

'That's very honourable of you.' She didn't try to hide the mockery in her words. Inside her head other words drummed—Why this man and no other? Why can't I get him out of my system?

The door to the back of the shop opened and Markus emerged. He said something to Chloe, glanced across at Hope and the man with her, then went into the office.

Of course Keir noticed. He said calmly, 'Come out to lunch with me, Hope, and we can talk then.'

His tone implied *If you don't, I'll stay here until I get the answers I want.* Blackmail, delivered with finesse and a ruthless determination to get his own way.

Hope picked up the necklace.

'Am I supposed to bristle and tell you I'm afraid of no one, then agree to go out with you?' she asked with spurious interest. 'Sorry, Keir, but I've grown beyond games like that.' She summoned the sort of smile mothers give to restless, fractious children, and finished kindly, 'It's been interesting to see you again. Enjoy the rest of your stay in Noosa.'

She'd hoped—expected!—to see another flash of temper light his eyes, but that sullen pleasure was denied.

Instead he looked down into her face and said in a voice that sent tiny shudders scudding the length of her spine, 'It's a shame to spoil such a satisfying moment for you, but I give you fair warning: I'll see you alone before I leave.'

He turned on his heel and walked out of the shop into the warm sunlight, a dark huntsman moving with a lithe, male grace that caught the eye of every woman in the street. Hope clamped her mouth shut and blinked fiercely, trying to banish his image from her cloudy brain.

'And what,' Chloe asked avidly, arriving far too late, 'was all that about?'

'I used to know him once,' Hope said bleakly. She picked up the pearls and carried them across to the window case. Her bones felt heavy, and when she tried to insert the key in the lock her hand shook, as though Keir had drained her of energy and will-power.

If it was a hundred years before she next saw him it would be too soon.

The older woman gave her a curious look. 'What's he like?'

'Tough, decisive, and a brilliant businessman,' Hope told her succinctly, resolutely refusing to look along the street.

Carefully she slid the pearls into the case, arranging them to show each precious sphere in the very best light. A passer-by stopped; sweat dampened her temples as she looked up, but the man who smiled at her didn't have ice-grey eyes or a face like a battle-hardened Adonis. She stepped back and closed the door and locked it.

From behind, Chloe said, 'He's also very, very rich and powerful—as in immensely, and seriously, and even *wickedly* powerful. Where did you meet him?'

Unemotionally Hope replied, 'He and my father were business associates. That was before the immense, serious and wicked bit, although he was already rich and powerful.'

'With a man like that in your past, it's no wonder poor Stewart didn't have a chance,' Chloe said with a spark of anger in her voice. 'He hasn't got what Keir Carmichael has.'

'Keir's got money,' Hope said contemptuously. 'Stewart's worth ten of him.'

'I know my brother's a lovely man, but he can't hold a candle to Mr Carmichael.' Chloe shrugged. 'And if you like Stewart so much, why did you send him away a week ago?'

Because she liked him so much; she'd tried so hard to love him, and it hadn't happened.

Hope turned away from the dazzle of Hastings Street and the infectious exuberance of the holiday-makers. 'It wasn't fair,' she said. 'I didn't want him to be unhappy.'

Chloe said quietly, 'He's not exactly happy now.'

'I know. I'm sorry.'

Stewart's sister shrugged and said fairly, 'Don't worry; he's not so far gone that he's miserable. He'll get over it.'

'Of course he will.' Hope changed the subject. 'Does Keir come here often? You obviously know him.'

Chloe shook her head. 'I read about him in some of Markus's business magazines and recognised him as soon as he came in the door.' She gave an envious smile. 'He's got a face that sticks in your memory—I'll bet it fuels a few erotic fantasies. According to one article, strategists around the Pacific Rim marvel at his energy and his business smarts and his luck.'

'If he's anything like most whizzkids he'll be bankrupt by the time he's forty—and so will a lot of the people who've trusted him with their money,' Hope retorted.

'He doesn't sound the sort to get himself into trouble. All control and command, with brains and guts and daring to back it up.' Chloe glanced sideways at Hope. 'You must have known him pretty well. You looked pretty thick while you were talking.'

A heated, forbidden pleasure ran surreptitiously through Hope. Ignoring it, she said in her most casual tone, 'Not very well at all.'

Chloe's eyes shifted. 'Really?' she asked sceptically. 'I wouldn't mind if someone as rich and charismatic as Keir Carmichael knew me as little as he seems to know you.'

Jealousy smoked through Hope's defences and stabbed her in the heart. 'He could choose any woman in the world,' she said curtly. 'Why would he be interested in me? Anyway, he's not a man any sensible woman wants to get tangled up with.'

'Rich men usually find beautiful women interesting! But I know what you mean. He's probably more than most women could handle. Though it'd be fun to go for the ride.' Chloe patted her smooth black hair and laughed reminiscently. 'He's such a hunk.'

'If you like them big and arrogant and overbearing,' Hope said with a snap.

Was Chloe crazy? There'd be no *fun* in an affair with Keir Carmichael; you didn't dice with the devil and expect to escape without losing your soul! Hope's skin tightened as she remembered dark words of passion spoken in a silent room, those long, tanned fingers on her skin, heat and fire and feverish, mindless lust...

Frustrated lust.

Keir had been ruthlessly clever, playing her like a particularly silly fish on his skilful, experienced line. Kisses, caresses, smouldering glances, sexy teasing until she'd been wild for him, unable to think, just a heap of quivering responses. Wanting him desperately, she'd offered herself in a hundred innocent ways, and he'd rejected her every time.

She'd thought him so honourable—until she'd overheard him with her father and found out that to both men she was just a pawn. Devastated, she'd sobbed hysterically to her mother, and for the first time ever Linda Sanderson had defied her husband's wishes and swiftly, secretly organised her daughter's escape from New Zealand. Less than twenty-four hours after that overheard conversation, Hope had been on a jet bound for London.

For a fleeting, depraved moment Hope toyed with an idea. Why not exact a little revenge for the shame and humiliation of four years ago? As soon as the idea reached her conscious mind she dismissed it; revenge was a rotten reason for doing anything.

Perhaps, she thought sardonically, walking across to the counter, she needed to exorcise Keir before she could allow herself to fall in love with any other man.

Temptation spread a lush cloak over her, clouding her brain. Why not use this unexpected meeting to put the past into perspective so that she could leave it behind her? Why not give in to this white-hot attraction, and so exorcise it?

A spasm of sensation contracted in the pit of her stomach, powering her heart-rate into hectic overdrive. Don't be an idiot, she told herself abruptly. Yes, Keir's still sexy as hell, but he's a hard, cold, mercenary robot.

Just like her father.

That knowledge would be an armour against disillusion if she—no! She would *not* meet him again.

But all that hot afternoon, as she smiled until her cheeks ached and sold enough pretty baubles to keep her boss happy, the thought reappeared, smooth as a snake, insidious, seductive.

Perhaps she could regain a little of her lost pride if she used Keir as he'd once tried to use her.

Revenge? Not revenge, she decided with grim desperation, but self-esteem. Although she'd spent the past four years trying to forget him, one look from his crystalline eyes and she'd surrendered again to that mindless enslavement of her senses.

Excitement rode her hard, glittered behind her lashes, hurried her breathing. When a couple of male customers gave her speculative glances she reimposed control, but behind her cool, helpful manner her body hummed with forbidden excitement and thoughts rushed feverishly through her head.

If she agreed to his demand for a meeting, was she asking for heartbreak? No; you had to love someone to have your heart broken, and she could never love Keir again. A meeting—a few minutes—wouldn't tip her life off its foundations...

She didn't want to be locked into this emotional and sexual prison for the rest of her life; she wanted to be able to look at Keir Carmichael with adult dispassion.

When the shop closed it didn't surprise her to find him waiting for her in the small alley at the rear.

In a pleasant tone that failed to hide the determination behind it, he said, 'Come for a drink with me, Hope.'

'All right,' she said calmly.

He took her to one of the bars that catered to tourists. 'I thought you'd prefer somewhere big and noisy and not at all intimate,' he observed. 'What would you like to drink?'

'Lime and soda, please.'

'Still as abstemious as ever.' He made it sound as though she hadn't changed at all.

I've got news for you, she thought. Four years has made a huge difference to me. It had given her an edge, an advantage, that Keir didn't understand.

A waiter materialised at Keir's elbow, took their orders and disappeared again. Ignoring the rest of the cheerfully informal bar, Keir asked evenly, 'Why did you leave Auckland so suddenly?'

Because of this man she'd woken alone on her twenty-third birthday in a rented room in a country not her own. It would be immensely satisfying to fling the words she'd overheard at him, to smash that seamless self-assurance.

But it would also reveal a humiliation that still made her feel sick and ashamed. Her only defence was pride.

'My mother thought it would be a good idea if I saw something of the world,' she said. 'I had a chance to go to England.'

'Without saying goodbye?'

Astonished, she glanced at his hard face. Mildly, because she had to tamp down her anger, she said, 'You left for America that day, if I remember correctly. I wrote to you.'

'A very stilted little note, thanking me for my kindness.'
He was watching her with narrowed, unsparing eyes.

A straggling group of men and women, obviously relishing
their freedom from children, came into the bar on a wave of
laughter and loud chatter. Shrugging, Hope said, 'I didn't
have much time to write.'

The drinks appeared. She took a grateful sip of the icy
refreshing lime and soda and looked up, keeping her eyes
shaded by her lashes, her expression carefully controlled.

'It must have been a sudden decision.' He paused, then
added, 'You hadn't said anything about an overseas trip.'

'The opportunity came up very quickly—a friend of my
mother's was going to London and decided she needed someone to go with her. It was too good a chance to miss.'

Keir lifted his long glass and downed some beer, throat
muscles working smoothly. How many times had she seen a
man drink? Hope thought despairingly. Probably hundreds;
she'd worked as a barmaid and waitress, even as a cook. Had
she ever felt that tight jag of hunger in her stomach with any
other man than Keir? She didn't even have to answer.

Every relationship—if they could be called that—she'd
embarked on had foundered on one simple thing. Hope liked
men; she found them attractive and fun and interesting—she
just didn't find them sexually appealing.

Except for this one.

Was she going to spend the rest of her life longing for the
man who had betrayed her?

Not if she could do something about it. It suddenly seemed
symbolic that today was her birthday; she'd wasted enough
time.

If *not* sleeping with Keir Carmichael had frozen her in a
virginal time warp, perhaps indulging her senses, sating herself with him until she could look at him without a quiver of
interest, might smash her a path to freedom.

The decision that had hidden slyly amongst her muddled

thoughts all afternoon emerged sharp and clear in her mind. If she seduced Keir and satisfied this forbidden, frustrated desire, she'd be able to put the past behind her, where it belonged.

Before, he'd been the one in control, the one who pulled the reins. This time she would make the decisions.

Hoping he'd read the heat along her cheekbones as a sign of excitement, not determination, and ignoring an age-old instinct that whispered frantically of danger, she said, 'So tell me what you've been doing these past years. Did you and my father finally come to some agreement about his firm?'

She held her breath and waited for the answer.

CHAPTER TWO

ANOTHER gale of laughter from the newcomers gusted through the bar. Heads turned, people smiled or looked disapproving, but Hope sat still, held prisoner by Keir's unreadable eyes.

'How did you know about that?' he asked in a detached voice that successfully concealed his emotions.

Hope lifted her shoulders in another shrug. 'My father said something about you buying into his business,' she returned casually.

'I didn't buy into it, I foreclosed on it,' Keir said, his tone matching hers, although an intriguing rasp gave the words an edge.

The conversation she'd overheard four years ago reverberated through her head, echoed in her ears with hideous clarity. 'He wouldn't have liked that.'

'No.'

In her letters her mother had never mentioned Keir's name, never indicated that her father had lost his firm, but Hope could imagine the repercussions at home, and shuddered inwardly. No one had guessed that James Sanderson had systematically terrorised his wife. Oh, he hadn't beaten her, but there were forms of abuse as bad as the physical.

Her mother's last years must have been hideous, and for that she could thank Keir.

Lowering her lashes, Hope watched the bubbles slide down the side of her tall glass and said in a brittle voice, 'Dull old business. Tell me about yourself. Are you married?'

A sardonic smile lifted the corners of Keir's mouth. 'No wife, no fiancée, no girlfriend.'

Opening her eyes very wide, she asked sweetly, 'What happened? There always used to be a very glamorous lover in your life.' She remembered the world-famous model, followed by a gloriously tempestuous Spanish opera singer—before her time, but carefully documented in the press.

She had to be careful; he was too experienced not to recognise fake flirtation. Probably she should just relax and let her treacherous body betray her all over again. It knew what it wanted, whereas she was discovering that her mind wanted something else entirely—to be able to trust him. Deciding to seduce Keir had not been easy; going about it was proving uncomfortably difficult.

His brows lifted. 'Not at the moment,' he said blandly. 'What about you? Any husband?'

'Not one.'

'Lover?'

She slid a sideways glance at him. 'You've already asked me that,' she told him softly. 'The answer's no.'

'Why were you so antagonistic in the shop?'

Thank heavens she'd thought up an answer to that. 'Shock, I think. You were the last person I expected to see.' Daringly she added, 'And a certain resentment; you didn't try to get in touch with me after I'd left New Zealand. I rather hoped you would.'

'I thought it best not to,' he said. 'You were very young.'

It was impossible to tell what he was thinking. Hope gave him a quick glance, then absently ran her finger around the top of her glass, concentrating on the whispering shimmer of sound. 'In other words,' she said dryly, 'I had a lot of growing up to do. You're right—I did.'

'That's not exactly what I meant.' But he didn't elaborate. Instead he said, 'I thought I'd see you at your mother's funeral.'

Something in his voice alerted her; she looked up to see his gaze on that slowly sliding finger. His mouth had hardened and the lick of colour along the high cheekbones startled her.

Hope stifled her first impulse to yank her hand away. Letting her finger continue its innocent glide around the rim, she said, 'I didn't know she'd died until a month after it happened.' She had to clear her throat before she could finish. 'I was working on a prawn boat out of Darwin.'

Keir said something under his breath and reached for the hand that had fallen away from her glass; as his fingers tightened around hers, heat and strength flowed through her in a surge of support that was as comforting as it was treacherous.

She said woodenly, 'Before I left she made me promise to write as often as I could, and to let her know where I was and what I was doing. Apparently it was a heart attack. I don't know whether she knew, but it was a—a shock to me.'

Quietly, uncompromisingly, Keir asked, 'Why did you leave New Zealand in such a hurry, Hope?' When Hope's hand twisted fiercely against his, his long fingers relaxed, freeing her.

Well, why not tell him, see what he said? The lime and soda slid down, wetting her parched throat before she was able to say, 'I resented my father's heavy-handed suggestion that I offer myself as a sacrificial virgin to save his position as CEO.'

Now would Keir admit his part in that infamous conversation?

His eyes turned into slivers of jagged ice. 'Did he suggest that?' he asked in a voice that sliced through her, dark with a focused, intense fury.

'Didn't he suggest it to you?'

She waited with locked breath.

Coolly disdainful, he avoided a direct answer. 'Why didn't you tell him to go to hell? You were eighteen, for heaven's sake, legally an adult—he had no control over you.'

Clever tactics—a brilliant evasion. Hope said curtly, 'My

mother suffered whenever I defied him.' Humiliated, she turned her head to look blindly around the bar.

A charged silence, emphasised by laughter and the subdued swish of cars on the street, crackled between them until it was broken by Keir's brutal, succinct oath. Every tiny hair on Hope's skin pulled upright.

'It wasn't too bad, really,' she said. 'Most of the time he just ignored me.'

'Your mother never said anything about it,' he said, something in his voice hinting at self-disgust.

'Who'd have believed her? My father was a brilliant actor, and by the time you came on the scene she was so worn down by his oppression that I think she'd forgotten what a normal life was. You walked into a real scorpions' nest when you came to our house. I had to get out, or he'd have made my mother's life an even worse hell.' She managed to summon a smile, tossed it at Keir's implacable, clever, deceitful face. 'I should thank you.'

'For ruining your life?'

'You didn't ruin my life,' she said, hiding her cynicism in a half-laugh. 'Leaving home was the best thing I could have done. I found out what freedom was like, and believe me, that would never have happened while I lived with my parents.'

A fugitive emotion glittered in the chilling depths of his eyes, but it was immediately leashed, overwhelmed by his smile. 'In that case, you owe me at least a dinner,' he said lazily, his voice smoothing over her jumpy nerves with the potency of a narcotic.

A douche of common sense almost doused the primal fire he'd lit with his sexual power. What the *hell* did she think she was doing? Courting disaster, that was what!

The bar was filling rapidly with people who'd spent the day doing the many things Noosa offered its visitors. Tanned, glowing, most of them wearing wealth and position with confidence, they were settling in to enjoy the evening. One of the men at the next table caught her eye and sent her a slow smile.

He was handsome, and that smile probably caused most women to shiver deliciously.

It did nothing to Hope.

She gave him a quick nod, then turned her attention back to the harsh features of the man who somehow kept her heart in purdah. Keir had seen the little byplay, of course, and was already directing a cold keep-off signal at the unfortunate man.

Fierce determination flowed through Hope, stiffening her bones. Before the end of the week she'd know what it was like to be Keir Carmichael's lover, and because no man could possibly meet four years' expectations, honed as they were by frustration and betrayal, she'd at last free herself from his potent male sorcery.

And if he thought a dinner date was going to end in sex—well, why not? They'd already gone through the courtship phase. But her pulses surged violently through her veins and sweat made the palms of her hands clammy.

'A friend of yours?' Keir asked, his voice cool and crisp.

'No,' she said calmly, 'but I'm sure he's a nice man.' A sly note of amusement slipped into her tone. 'Actually, I owe you much more than a dinner.' Was that too suggestive? Keeping her lashes lowered, she hurried on, 'However, I'm going to be busy tonight.'

Keir's black brows lifted. 'An unbreakable appointment?'

She shuddered. 'I have to model a necklace.' She was almost going to add, But tomorrow night I'm free. Fortunately discretion leashed the words before they escaped.

'Then how about tomorrow night?' Keir asked a little too smoothly.

Back in the shop it had seemed so simple, like a prescription: *Keir Carmichael. To be taken as needed for fever in the blood and generalised loss of interest in other men.*

Except that if she made love with Keir it would change her life, and Hope didn't know that she was ready for that.

She breathed deeply until the spinning panic was under control. Wasn't that the whole point of the exercise—to change her life, free her from the hangover of her childish infatuation and set her on a new path to the future?

Firmly, without giving herself time to dither, she said, 'I'd like that. What time and where?'

'Seven, and wear casual clothes.'

'In Noosa everyone goes casual. Do you mean casual casual or chicly expensive casual?' And if he said chic, she'd whip into a certain boutique and spend money she couldn't afford on the outfit that had been tormenting her deliciously from the window.

His smile was sardonic. 'What's the difference?'

'Denim shorts and a T-shirt, or floaty white linen designer resort wear?' she asked with a sweet smile, reaching for her glass.

His brows lifted. 'Shorts,' he said smoothly.

As she sipped more lime and soda, a slow curl of apprehension mixed with wildfire anticipation when she saw him watch her mouth.

Yes, she thought, trying to be exultant. Yes, he was definitely interested...

She set the glass down on the table and got to her feet. 'Lovely,' she said, her breath catching as he rose and looked down at her with a smile that shafted down her spine and literally curled her toes. 'What time?'

'Make it eight o'clock.'

'Who's the dude in the London tailoring?' the bodyguard asked, staring across the hotel reception room.

One appalled glance revealed that Hope's guardian angel

had let her down again; producing Keir at the prestigious Chef of the Year award was viciously unfair. Especially as she couldn't sneak out. Apart from the difficulty of avoiding notice with the seductive swaying glide caused by four-inch heels, she had responsibilities.

'Keir Carmichael,' she muttered, resisting the urge to clap her hand over the necklace that hung conspicuously around her throat. Even if she hid it, there was still the blatant dress. And the sexy shoes...

Pulses drumming to a surge of adrenalin, she switched her gaze to the members of the string quartet, playing Mozart with the resigned expressions of men who understood they were merely the background music. Why on earth *hadn't* she expected Keir? This was the sort of occasion he probably got asked to all the time.

The bodyguard nodded in a satisfied way. 'The number one merchant banker. I heard he was in town. Officially he's on holiday, but someone said he's meeting a group of Chinese policy makers.'

Clearly the rumour mill was in full production. Despising herself, Hope said, 'I wonder why.'

The bodyguard's massive shoulders lifted. 'Setting up some sort of deal. Whatever it is, there'll be money in it. You should flaunt that necklace at him—he might be in the mood to buy.'

'I'm not flaunting anything,' Hope said tightly.

Grinning, the bodyguard said, 'Coulda fooled me,' but was professional enough not to let his eyes wander over her exposed shoulders, or down to the stocking-clad thigh revealed by the slit skirt.

Hot with anger and embarrassment for allowing herself to be bulldozed into this ridiculous situation, Hope realised with ignoble relief that Keir wasn't with the woman who'd bought the goanna pin. He didn't appear to be with anyone.

Ignoring the women who eyed him with avid fascination,

he stopped just inside the door and looked around with a cool self-confidence that set her teeth on edge.

'Knows how to make himself felt, doesn't he?' the body-guard said admiringly. 'Amazing what money can do for you.'

Keir's presence had little to do with his income. Of course, Hope thought, struggling to be objective, tall men had the same unfair advantage as beautiful women. And he knew how to dress. In a room full of expensively gowned women and superbly tailored men, his evening clothes were a marvel of spare restraint. That they showed off with tantalising fidelity his broad shoulders and lean, lithely muscled body, narrow hips and long legs helped—but didn't entirely explain—his commanding, forceful dominance.

A woman approached him, a woman who smiled and displayed her interest in a thousand unspoken, easily read signals. Rank jealousy jagged through Hope. Don't even *try* flirting with him, she silently advised the woman. He might look like the dark lord of Hades' very sexy brother, but he's much, much tougher.

Besides, he's going to be busy with me.

Using will-power to prise her teeth apart, Hope said curtly, 'Don't you think the raw material might have some small effect on the way he looks?'

'You reckon?' The bodyguard eyed Keir with interest. 'Nah, he's in good shape underneath the clothes, but he's no oil painting; it has to be the money. Women really chase rich dudes.'

'Are you saying all women go after men purely for their money?' Hope asked with spurious pleasantness, taking her anger and hollow panic out on the man. Feeling mean didn't stop her from adding snidely, 'Can't you get a girlfriend?'

He shot her a resentful look. 'I don't have any trouble,' he said shortly, 'but then, I'm better-looking than Carmichael.'

Keir's hard, compellingly masculine face with its bold symmetry, the sharp contrast between dark hair and skin and crystalline eyes, made descriptions such as 'handsome' or 'good-looking' irrelevant. It was his unconscious air of competence and authority—allied to his prowling, potent sexuality—that attracted women.

But Hope was already regretting her unusual spite. She agreed peaceably, 'Yes, you are.'

As though Keir felt her scrutiny, he looked up; their eyes clashed, duelled across the room. Hope's breath was stopped in her lungs by a discharge of energy so electric she wondered why people weren't ducking.

Keir nodded to her with a slight smile that simmered through her blood, tightening her skin in an atavistic instinct as old as danger. She answered the mocking challenge with a blank face and a non-committal tilt of her head. Her precarious dress—worth, so her boss had informed her, over five thousand dollars—chose that moment to surrender to gravity and slide off her shoulder.

Anchoring it with a fast clutch, she eased the glinting, shimmering silk into place and began to breathe again, as shallowly as she could without fainting. If she could have clapped her heels together and disappeared, she'd have been home instantly. Until Keir arrived she'd been enjoying herself—mostly—but now the noisy party, suffered in the close, unaffectionate company of a bodyguard, became intolerable.

Not too far away Markus Bravo—her boss and instigator of this charade—was taking a keen interest in the welfare of his stock while chatting up the glitterati. It had been his idea to dress her in amber silk and load her with the hundred thousand dollars worth of diamonds that Keir had eyed with such distaste in the salon.

'There are going to be television crews from all over Australia,' he'd informed her with a manic gleam. 'These food awards are big time!'

Horrified, she'd objected, 'Foodies spend all their money on food and wine and the latest woks; they don't buy diamonds. And strolling around a party wearing a vulgar necklace isn't part of my job description, so hire a model!'

'Harry Forsayth will be there,' Markus said cunningly.

'Who?'

Disappointed, Markus told her, 'Only the most famous film star Australia's ever produced! He's going to present the prizes because his father used to have a seafood restaurant in Noosa. That was before he drank himself to death, of course.'

'The film star…? Oh, you mean his *father*!' After a quick shake to clear her head, Hope tried again. 'Why on earth should Harry Forsayth want to buy this ghastly necklace? You need a millionaire at least.'

Or a billionaire…

Markus glowered. 'Most millionaires look after their money too carefully. Film stars spend—especially when they still can't believe their luck. And Harry is the sort to spend up big—even when he was just a good-looking kid, only interested in surfing and girls, he had to have the best board and the prettiest girl. He'll want those diamonds as soon as he sees them. Come on, Hope, be a sport! Of course you'll get paid well for it.'

Flicking the necklace with a disparaging finger, she muttered, 'Model's rates?'

Sensing surrender, he grinned. 'You're not a model.' But he named a sum that would bring the laptop computer she wanted almost within her reach. And a laptop with internet access would make it so much easier to produce the travel articles she was slowly building a name with.

When Hope still shook her head he added hastily, 'And commission if it sells, of course. A percentage deal.'

Tempted by sordid money, Hope frowned. 'Why don't you just cut your losses and get the stones reset into smaller pieces? Then you might be able to sell them without parading me around like a horse in the sale ring.'

'You sound just like Narelle,' Markus snapped. In a high-pitched imitation of his wife's voice he went on, '"Markus, admit for once that you made a mistake. You should never have bought the necklace. When anyone in Noosa wants to spend a hundred thousand dollars they automatically go to the old family jeweller in Sydney or London or New York. They won't spend it here."' He snorted and resumed his own voice. 'She was right, damn her.'

'Except for pearls,' Hope said fairly. For some reason pearls sold in spite of their price. Perhaps it was the seaside ambience.

With an extravagant gesture Markus dismissed pearls. 'Harry Forsayth will have Lisette Parish with him. He's been romancing her for at least a month. And she has an eye for large stones. When she left that other guy she was living with she took a couple of million dollars' worth of jewels with her. And there will be—' he held up his hand when Hope opened her mouth '—there will be others at this do, too. Very rich others. When they see you, a beautiful woman, dressed by—oh, a top designer—'

Mistaking Hope's small yelp of alarm for excitement, he added hastily, 'Well-insured, of course! Anything—*every-thing*,' he amended with aplomb, 'looks brilliant on you. You've got an inbuilt style that will carry even this neckpiece off.'

She eyed him consideringly. 'I might do it if you tell me why you're so determined to sell it as it is.'

He wriggled, but finally confessed, 'Oh, all right. I've got a bet on with Narelle. If my sales top hers this quarter we go to Monte Carlo for the Grand Prix.'

Although they were a very happy couple, Narelle and Markus were fiercely competitive; lately, some inspired marketing had boosted Narelle's fashion salon to new heights.

'I see,' Hope said. 'And if she wins?'

'Paris for the collections,' he said dismally. Then he'd leaned forward and persevered, 'Hope, if you wear the necklace I know we can sell it. Someone'll want it.'

It seemed that he'd been right. Fastened into an outrageously sexy dress created by an *avant garde* couturier in Sydney, her hair done as a favour by the top hairdresser on the Sunshine Coast, her face made up by the local expert, Hope had already given three people the name of Markus's shop, and with as much grace as she could muster had dealt with a variety of men who'd ogled her without any attempt at subtlety.

Not, she thought bitterly, that she looked at all subtle; the flimsy silver wire that was supposed to hold the dress together—and on—wasn't up to the job. The superb Italian sandals with their elegant, ridiculous heels were as provocative as footwear could be. And the necklace shouted its presence. She should charge Markus danger and inconvenience money.

If she managed to sell the wretched thing she was going to earn every cent of the commission.

And here came another middle-aged inconvenience, leering at her with the sort of smile that proclaimed his thoughts as clearly as a poster.

'Well, well, well, you're a pretty little parcel,' he said thickly. He'd drunk just enough to slip the reins on his control.

Keeping her voice cool, Hope stepped back. 'What a *novel* compliment.'

A female voice from behind him called him. He hesitated, then gave Hope another ogling smile before turning. A thin blonde woman, exquisitely dressed, surveyed Hope with scornfully raised eyebrows before grasping his arm with the speed of long practice; talking quickly, she inserted both of them into a group a few paces away.

As well as danger and inconvenience money, Hope decided vengefully, she'd charge Markus disdain money. He'd end up without any profit at all.

'You're supposed to protect me,' she muttered at the security guard.

'Lady, I'm here to make sure no one snatches the jewels, and he didn't have his hands anywhere near your neck,' he said, grinning. 'Anyway, you're more than capable of looking after yourself.'

She gave him a haughty glare and turned, only to find herself staring up into Keir's harshly cut features. The impact of those arctic eyes snatched her breath away and sent her heart into a frenzy.

Not that he was looking at her. No, he was drilling the security guard with a narrowed, intent stare while he said pleasantly, 'Introduce your friend, Hope.'

The bodyguard blurted, 'I'm no friend of hers, mate. I'm here to make sure no one takes off with the jewellery.' He pronounced it 'joolery'. 'Or the dress,' he added. 'That's not hers either.'

Hope could have killed him, especially when Keir made a leisurely inspection of the dress, lingering on the expanses of skin it revealed. Heat flickered up from her breasts, setting fire to her throat and face, turning inward to melt her bones, but she faced him with lifted chin and a taunting little smile.

Keir said thoughtfully, 'I have no intention of removing either.'

The guard eyed him with caution, but felt honour-bound to point out, 'You'd say that anyway.'

Hope repressed a gulp of laughter.

Markus Bravo came striding up. 'Everything all right?' he asked, drawing himself up to his full five foot seven.

'Yes.' Keir spoke indolently, not trying to hide the warning note beneath the word.

Embarrassed, Hope saw the moment her boss realised who

he was speaking to; strutting wariness was replaced by an eager cupidity that made her feel ill. Did Keir's bank account mean that he dealt with this sort of servility every day?

Serves him right, she thought stoutly.

'Enjoying yourself, Mr Carmichael?' her boss asked, beaming as he tried to urge Hope forward. 'Have you met my assistant Hope Sanderson, a New Zealander like yourself?'

'Hope and I have known each other for years,' Keir said, a humourless smile just touching his mouth at Markus's astonished reaction to that bit of information.

'A very long time ago,' Hope said in her most wooden tone.

Nothing could shake Keir's aloof, cynical self-sufficiency. The security guard—in lurk mode a few steps away—was doing his best not to be impressed. Balked by Hope's stubborn refusal to move closer to Keir, Markus was now trying to edge her beneath the chandelier, so that the lights could pick up the diamonds around her throat, his reproachful glare indicating that any assistant of his who knew a billionaire should have been steering said billionaire towards the shop instead of hiding the information.

As exposed as the fairy on a Christmas tree, Hope allowed herself to be positioned beneath the shimmering crystals. That was, after all, why she was there.

'So you know each other!' Markus almost simpered. 'Well, New Zealand's a tiny country—I suppose everyone knows everyone else.' Summoning what he probably thought was another benign smile, he went on with a transparent lack of truth, 'Oh, the Princess has just waved at me! I must go— wonderful to meet you, Mr Carmichael. I do hope you enjoy your stay in our lovely little town.' Still beaming, he abandoned them for a woman with improbable hair the same colour as her pink dress.

Black brows met for a moment above Keir's cool eyes. 'The Princess?' he asked.

'I think she used to be the fourth wife of a minor member of some exiled Balkan royal family,' Hope explained. 'When the fifth wife took her place she couldn't be persuaded to give up the title.'

You couldn't call his look contemptuous; it was more the sardonic understanding of a man who expects nothing from anyone. For some strange reason it both exasperated Hope and made her profoundly sorry for him.

Obscurely compelled to defend the woman, Hope said, 'It's an innocent delusion.'

Keir's lashes drooped. 'Delusions are never innocent.'

Although the bodyguard had melted into the crowd as inconspicuously as someone with a neck wider than his head could, he wasn't too far away. Coward, Hope thought, but didn't blame him. Keir Carmichael was more than intimidating. Tension pulled her nerves, tightened her muscles until her spine stiffened.

'Hello there,' a male voice said loudly from behind. Groping hands ran across her shoulder and a blast of alcohol-scented breath met her nostrils as the voice asked, 'How much are you charging for this gorgeous thing, then?'

In a voice soft and menacing as the hiss of lightning across a thunder-dark sky, Keir ordered, 'Get your hands off her.'

CHAPTER THREE

THE intruder jerked away, and Hope was left standing alone in a cold, echoing cone of emptiness until Keir's lean, elegant hand closed with shocking power around her arm.

She was appalled at the comfort she gained from his hard warmth and primal strength. But infinitely more dangerous was her violent physical reaction—like being enveloped in a firestorm of mindless sensation where nothing counted except her body's fierce response to his heat and sexual potency.

Above the string quartet and the babble of conversation that hadn't really died she heard the other man's voice, startled and a little truculent.

'It's all right, mate, I didn't mean the lady any harm. My old friend Markus told me the necklace was for sale, and I thought I'd take a look at it.' He spoke with a hybrid Australian-American accent.

The film star, Harry Forsayth? Hope drew in a deep breath, but before she could answer Keir said in an even voice, 'You can look.' His expression finished the warning—*But don't touch.*

'Yeah, OK, no problems.' The other man sounded disconcerted.

And no wonder. Although Keir hadn't raised his voice, it was charged with a taut warning. The bodyguard had appeared just behind the film star, and people were beginning to turn and stare.

Hope tore herself away from the painful pleasure of Keir's support and said, 'I'm sorry, it was just that you startled me.'

'Hey, wouldn't want to do that. I'm the one who's sorry.'

Relief coloured the film star's voice and he deliberately exaggerated the last word.

Harry Forsayth was more handsome than any man had a right to be, yet beside Keir he dwindled into a dim imitation. Once certain of Hope's attention, he dropped his eyelid in a lazy wink, clearly expecting a dazzled response.

Unstirred, she said in a matter-of-fact tone, 'That's all right.'

'Perhaps I'll come and see Markus at the shop,' Harry Forsayth said, frowning slightly as his eyes left her face and travelled to that of the man beside her. He gave Keir a man-to-man nod. 'No offence, mate, I didn't know she was taken.'

The smile vanished from Hope's face. Outraged, she noticed the bodyguard's respectful look when Keir replied with hard assurance, 'In future it might be a good idea to find out first.'

A dinner-jacketed man—a professional minder judging by his ready-for-anything expression—shouldered his way through the crowd.

Harry looked at him, then stuck out his hand to Keir. 'Been nice meeting you,' he said. After they'd shaken he looked across at Hope and subjected her to a slow, significant, completely unimportant smile. 'Nice meeting you,' he repeated, and left them.

Aware of the covert glances, the hum of speculative conversation, Hope struggled to regain her composure with all the grace of a warrior scrambling into an ill-fitting suit of armour.

'I gather this is your boss's idea of a good marketing ploy,' Keir observed in a tone cold enough to sink the *Titanic* without need of an iceberg.

Hope shrugged, remembering too late her suicidal dress. Grimly clutching the wandering material against her breasts in what she hoped was a nonchalant manner, she said, 'It seemed like a good idea at the time.'

'Possibly.' Wintry eyes slid with incandescent effect over her exposed skin. 'However, he chose the wrong clothes. No one is looking at that necklace; they're too busy wondering if *you're* for sale. And with good reason—that thing reveals every asset you have.'

His voice didn't alter, but his contempt cut as sharply as if he'd shouted it at her.

Grateful for the layers of cosmetics so skilfully applied, Hope took a deep breath, forcing her anger into studied formality. Eyes glittering, she tried to sting in her turn. 'Thanks for the compliment, although I like to believe that I have more than physical assets. And I'm not—and never have been—for sale.'

A muscle flicked in Keir's strong jawline; tanned skin tightened across high, arrogant cheekbones, and fierce control thinned his mouth. 'Then I'm surprised you agreed to make such an exhibition of yourself,' he said with silky, damning precision.

Colour flared through her skin. After a slashing, furious glare she turned away.

His hand curved around the fragile bones of her shoulder, stopping her. 'I'm sorry,' he said unexpectedly. 'That was uncalled for.'

When Hope pulled away he released her, leaving the unseen imprint of his fingers burning into her flesh. 'I don't plan to dignify it with an answer,' she returned sweetly.

His eyes acknowledged the hit. 'Your eyes still shoot sparks when you're angry,' he murmured.

Controlling a flagrant urge to slap his amused face, she relaxed her tense fingers and said with syrupy enthusiasm, 'Did you know that eyes don't change, either in colour or expression? It's the movement of the little muscles in our faces that make them appear to. So although mine may look as though they spit sparks, it's just an illusion.'

She surprised a laugh out of him. 'Like so much else,' he

said. His expression changed as his pale gaze came to rest with disturbing intensity on her mouth. For a moment he looked predatory, pagan. 'What about your mouth, Hope? Do tiny muscles make it soften and ripen when I look at it? Or is it telling me that you're wanting me to kiss you as much as I want to kiss you?'

'No!' she exclaimed, folding her lips into a straight line that banished any softness.

A missed opportunity, she realised instantly. She should have flirted with him then, fluttered her lashes at him, made it plain that she wanted him. Trying to salvage something, she said, 'And you have too much control to...'

The words faded into nothingness when he touched her bottom lip with his thumb, running it lightly, tantalisingly along the margin between mouth and skin.

Hope's heart threatened to crash through her ribs. Mutely she stared into the silvery depths of his eyes and saw hunger there, a lick of cold fire that burned into her heart and her body.

Fortunately a waitress, blonde hair bouncing around her shoulders, offered a tray of champagne. 'A drink, madam?' she asked, watching Keir's hand drop to his side. Her swift glance at Hope said, *You lucky thing!*

Hope accepted a glass, hiding behind its fragile protection while the waitress turned to Keir. Hope watched with a connoisseur's eye as the woman was treated to his smile. Flushing, she croaked, 'A glass of champagne, sir?'

What would it be like to know you had that effect on most people you met? No wonder Keir's confidence was bone-deep.

'No, thank you,' he said, and waited until the waitress had wobbled away before continuing, 'Your touching faith in my control is baseless; beauty is the most powerful weapon in the whole armoury between the sexes, and I'm far from immune to it. You were dangerously lovely when I first knew you; you're even more so now that you've grown up, golden and rich and exotic, a peach for plucking.'

The sensation scorching through every cell in her body was fed by his tone, by the twist of his chiselled mouth and the way he looked at her; for an exhilarating, terrifying second Hope read naked desire in his face.

She drew in a sharp breath, only to make another wild grab at the wretched dress as it began to slither downwards again. Keir's lashes drooped.

Tartly Hope said, 'You make me sound like fruit past its use-by date.'

His mouth twitched. 'You don't need to manufacture defences, Hope. I'm not pressuring you.'

Silence—taut, echoing—stretched between them. Lifting her head, she asked thinly, 'Why did you come to Noosa?'

'To see you, of course.'

He was a very good liar. Thin-lipped, Hope dragged her gaze away and caught Markus staring at her, his brows meeting above his splendid nose.

She said tersely, 'A likely story. Now, if you'll excuse me, I have to mingle. Perhaps you should, too. There must be plenty of people here who'd love to talk to you. You should take what profit you can from the evening.'

Keir's mouth compressed; he said in a voice that came too close to being bored, 'Unfortunately I have another appointment.' Above a quick, ruthless smile, thick lashes screened his eyes. 'I'll leave you to continue selling. Goodnight.'

She clamped her teeth together as he turned and padded away with the swift, lithe grace she'd never forgotten. Hope turned to the security guard, who'd reappeared like a determined beetle.

He said aggrievedly, 'There's no need to glower at me like that. It's not my fault if you've had a fight with your boyfriend.'

'He's *not* my boyfriend.'

'Looked like it from where I was,' he muttered.

Keir's departure left her wrung out yet elated, like a swordsman who'd fought a worthy opponent and lost. In the barren years since that volatile excitement had last ripped through her life, she'd tried desperately to forget the spell Keir cast when he smiled at her, when he touched her, when his voice deepened on her name.

Perhaps she was addicted to dominant men. Perhaps she was co-dependent, or whatever the latest term was. Perhaps her childhood had imprinted her with an unhealthy need...

No, she'd met plenty of other arrogant men—the world was full of them—and they'd all left her completely cold. Only Keir had such a devastating effect on her.

Well, she was going to deal with that.

What 'other appointment' did Keir have?

After another hour, during which Hope, the jewels and the dress paraded the room, Markus finally decided to call an end to the farce. Thankfully, she went back to the shop with him and the bodyguard, took off the diamonds, shed the dress in the workaday restroom and resumed her own clothes, a T-shirt and trousers in tawny cotton.

'Do you want a lift home?' Markus asked her as he locked the shop—already, she could see, anticipating the pleasure of telling his wife that Harry Forsayth was probably going to buy the necklace.

'No, thanks. It's only a couple of kilometres, and I could do with some fresh air.'

He nodded. 'See you tomorrow—oh, it's your day off, isn't it? Enjoy it, then.'

His car purred away, closely followed by the bodyguard's, and Hope began to walk along the elegant, leafy street that backed Noosa's famous Main Beach.

Hastings Street hummed day and night; restaurants and bars and cafés buzzed with conversation, and people strolled the well-lit pavement eyeing the clothes in the expensive boutiques, enjoying the simple pleasure of being there. Lights shone in the windows of hotels and apartments, and the sound of laughter almost covered the dry rustle of wind-tossed palm fronds.

Hope sniffed at the freshness of greenery and salt air, enjoying it after the mingled scents of expensive perfumes and aftershaves, of cosmetics and alcohol that had marked the reception.

A man coming in the opposite direction smiled at her; Hope nodded back, but kept her expression serious and her feet moving.

Nevertheless he stopped as he said, 'Great evening, isn't it?'

'Lovely,' she replied, and walked briskly by.

After a few unfortunate experiences she'd learned to surround herself with invisible barriers; even against the men she knew wanted more than the casual friendliness which was all she seemed able to give them. Chloe's brother Stewart had been a mistake; she'd liked him so much, only to hurt him when she hadn't been able to respond to his caresses.

Surely if she got Keir out of her system she'd be able to fall in love? She wanted a man who'd laugh with her and talk with her, have the same values—someone she could respect, someone who respected her.

A man without a dominant bone in his body.

She stopped to look in the window of an art gallery. Her eyes roamed fretfully over portraits of brilliant reef fish, skilfully composed—but once you'd seen one Scarlet Trumpeter in pellucid blue water with the sun's rays dazzling limpidly through it, you'd seen them all.

The oldest instinct of all shouted a silent warning; in the window glass she saw a dark shape moving behind her. With swift confidence she swivelled, automatically assuming a ready position.

'Relax, you're not in danger.' Keir spoke with cool assurance as he noted her hands, prepared to deliver a stunning blow, and her stance—poised, alert, watchful.

Adrenalin drove the blood through her veins, banishing both her tiredness and the slight melancholy that had gripped her. Although she straightened up, she didn't move towards him.

'Were you trying to frighten me?' she asked curtly.

'No. I saw you from the taxi.'

Her eyes slid past him to note the cab at the kerb. 'So?' she challenged.

'So I wondered why you were walking down the street by yourself.'

Hope quenched a treacherous flame deep inside her. 'It's perfectly safe.'

'No place is perfectly safe for a woman at this time of night. Your employer could at least have sent you home in a taxi.'

'Markus knows I can look after myself.'

There was an electric second's pause before he asked, 'Because you've had to show him? Is that why you learned self-defence?'

'Markus?' She managed a laugh, short and unamused. 'No, he's not a harasser—he's very happily married.'

Keir's frown didn't lessen. 'I'm almost at my hotel—I'll walk the rest of the way. Get into the taxi. The driver can take you home.' When she didn't answer he added, 'Unless you want me to walk home with you—or just behind you.'

Anger and a simmering frustration boiled into resentment. '*That's* harassment, which happens to be illegal in Australia.'

'In New Zealand, too, but I doubt whether anyone would consider it harassment if I told the cab-driver to stay with you all the way.' His tone made it obvious that this was as far as he was prepared to compromise.

Knowing it was surrender, Hope said aloofly, 'Then I'll go in the cab, but I'll pay my way.'

'If you must,' Keir said, no softness warming the harsh strength of his features.

After Hope had given the driver her address, the woman set the cab in motion and observed in a voice filled with purely female interest, 'Your boyfriend didn't like seeing you on the street.'

'He most definitely isn't my boyfriend.' It felt as though she'd been saying that all night. Anyway, the word was wrong; Keir was far too much man to qualify as a boyfriend. A lover, oh, yes...

Hastily she broke into that train of thought. 'I don't really know him.'

Because the Keir she'd adored with all the fervour of her innocent heart had not been the man who'd said to her father, 'All right, let's deal.'

'You might not know him, but he certainly knows you,' the driver said, smiling.

'A little,' Hope admitted reluctantly, repressing the desire to ask the driver where she'd picked Keir up. Where he'd spent the two hours since he'd left the reception was none of her business.

The cab swung through a roundabout and headed towards Noosa Junction. 'Take my advice,' the driver said, 'and let him win now and then.'

'Men who have to win became unfashionable when my mother was young.'

'Think so, love? There'll always be masterful men, and it doesn't mean you have to knuckle under, you know. Most of 'em like a strong woman to match them. He's got an interesting face, that one, and he's pleasant with the hired help.'

Trenchantly Hope said, 'I should hope so.'

The driver laughed, a comfortable middle-aged, experienced sound. 'And sexy,' she said, drawling the word. 'It helps. He was made to be king of the heap, your non-boyfriend. They're not easy to live with, men like that, but they make great husbands and lovers.'

'You sound as though you know.'

'I married one. We had fifteen fantastic years together until he got killed five years ago.' At Hope's small distressed sound she shrugged. 'I survived, even though I still miss him every day. We used to fight—man, did we fight!—but he was always there for me and I was there for him, and we laughed a lot more than we fought. A mate like that keeps your heart in good shape.'

The taxi drew into the kerb. As the woman accepted the fare she said, 'Ever studied body language?'

'Well—no.'

'A dollar change.' She handed the coin over. 'Taxi-drivers learn a lot from their fares. You can take it from me. He's after you and he's pretty sure you're not going to tell him to go to hell. If you don't want anything to come of it, you'd better ride out of Noosa as soon as you can.'

She gave another rich chuckle and the car drew away, leaving Hope looking after it with a primitive shiver of apprehension.

'Oh, rubbish,' she muttered, almost running up the narrow path to unlock her door. Sniffing distastefully at the warm, slightly musty air inside, she switched on the fan and pushed back the windows behind their security grilles before going into the bathroom to clean off the elaborate, masterfully applied make-up. Her fingertip traced a small scar, white and thin, scarcely visible after all these years.

She'd been five when her mother's diamond ring had snicked from her mouth to her chin, a shallow cut that had healed into this fine line.

That was when she'd learned, once and for all, that dominant men were not safe.

Early the next morning Hope woke with a stuffy head and eyes so gritty they felt as though someone else had over-used them the previous night. The memories that had haunted her sleep—of loving Keir with mindless intensity and praying that he might love her, of betrayal and bitter disillusion—hung like shrouds over her mood.

Muttering, she flung back the duvet and stretched, listening to the loud calls of those other early risers the birds. A run through the cool grey dawn followed by a swim at Main Beach would banish the stale leftovers of a past love affair.

She pulled shorts and a misty green and gold shirt over her swimming suit, grabbed up a towel and locked the door behind her.

'Hey, Hope!'

Two faces, belonging to a boy of ten and his eight-year-old sister, peered through the bare stems of the frangipani tree on the boundary. Her landlady, who lived on the upper floor of the house, had planted that tree forty years before; its surreal grey branches were waiting for the warmer touch of spring to coax forth big clusters of leaves and satin-smooth flowers, cream and gold, and sweetly, intensely perfumed.

'Hope,' Jaedan said urgently, 'can we come with you?'

'Ask your parents.'

He pulled a hideous face. 'They said that unless it was bleeding or broken or there were flames involved we weren't to wake them up.'

Sympathetically Hope shook her head. 'Sorry.'

They sighed in concert. 'OK,' Abby said cheerfully. 'We'll watch the cartoons, or I might make pancakes. That usually wakes them up.'

''Specially when you burn them,' her brother retorted smartly.

Hope grinned as she waved to them and swung down the road. During the time she'd spent in Noosa she'd become close friends with the Petrie family. She'd miss them.

With a shock she realised that the decision to move on had

been simmering beneath her conscious thoughts ever since she'd seen Keir again.

'You're running scared,' she said out loud, startling a family of crimson and ultramarine rosellas that were squabbling over the scarlet flowers of a bottlebrush.

The taxi-driver's voice popped into her mind. *If you don't want anything to come of it, you'd better ride out of Noosa as soon as you can.*

A hot little shiver slithered the length of her spine. Four years ago Keir might have seen her only as a means to an end, but that wasn't how he looked at her now. No longer naïve and stupefied by love, she recognised the glitter of sexual awareness in his eyes.

Three sedate, dowagerish black and white pelicans flew towards the river. Pushing Keir from her mind, Hope eased into a smooth run, concentrating on the crisp scent of eucalyptus trees and the cool, fresh air.

She'd expended enough useless emotional energy and angst on the imperious—and, for a frozen moment when Harry Forsayth had let his hands wander, *lethal*—Keir Carmichael. She had no intention of wasting a moment of this glorious morning by obsessing any further over him!

The beach stretched before her, slicked by the tide, a curved pale crescent almost empty of people. Even the volleyball jocks hadn't arrived yet, although a few family groups were picking out the best spots.

As Hope looked around for a suitable place to dump her bag, an elderly matriarch called out from beneath her sun umbrella, 'Leave it with us, love. We'll make sure no one steals it.'

'Thanks very much.'

Hope stuffed her shorts and shoes into the bag, handed it over, and ran down to the sea.

Gasping at the bracing slickness of the water against her heated skin, she dived into the waves in one neat movement and struck out for the horizon, driven by a restless compulsion.

Although she was fit and an excellent swimmer, her legs were shaking with over-use when at last she staggered out of the water. Scared by her stupidity, she stood breathing heavily, painfully, with the sun beating down on her unprotected shoulders.

'What the hell were you doing? Trying to drown yourself?' a furious male voice enquired as Keir strode across the sand.

Struggling to control her panting, she said, 'Of course not.'

'You're exhausted.' He hooked his arm around her heaving shoulders and urged her further up the beach.

'And good morning to you, too,' Hope replied on a harsh intake of breath, trying to ignore the ragged thunder of her heart in her ears. 'I swam a bit too far, but I'm fine.' When he didn't immediately let her go she jerked away. 'Thank you.'

He stood back a step, anger glittering in the ice-grey depths of his eyes. 'You damned near drowned yourself. I saw you from my window and got down here so fast I probably scorched a furrow in the floor.'

'I didn't realise how far out I'd gone. It's all right; I don't make a practice of it.' Her breasts lifted and fell as she dragged more air into her straining lungs. 'I won't do it again.'

'I thought every beach in Australia had bronzed lifesavers watching out for those stupid enough to swim outside the flags.' His caustic tone burned her ears. 'Where are they?'

Hope rubbed her hands down her arms, noting with feverish, unbidden satisfaction that his eyes followed the betraying movement. 'They'll be here in a fortnight, when the season starts.'

Emotion ran in a turbulent rip beneath the banal words. Forcing her weighted legs to move, she set off up the beach.

'You need a keeper,' Keir said, barely reining in his aggression as he kept pace. 'Look at you—you can barely put one leg in front of the other. Where are your clothes?'

Nodding at the family party, she told him.

'Stay here while I get them.'

Women of the cab-driver's generation, Hope thought sourly, might call him a masterful man. She called him uncompromising and dictatorial.

It wasn't fair that he was also sinfully, dangerously attractive. Her eyes followed the sun-summoned blue flames in his black hair, lingered on a cotton shirt in shades of ice-blue and grey, picked out well-muscled thighs concealed by trousers in a darker shade of grey. Hot sensation clenched her stomach at his lithe, unhurried ease, all masculine grace and the latent promise of great strength and endurance.

Smiling, he stopped and spoke to the family spread out on their rugs. They all sat up, interested, alert. After he'd spoken, the older woman looked past him; Hope lifted her hand and waved, although she knew her gesture wasn't necessary. Keir's personal sorcery—that compelling, powerful presence—had had its usual effect.

Without demur the family surrendered her bag. Hope shivered as a slight breeze plucked at her, chilling her flesh. Beneath the thin material of her bathing suit her nipples puckered embarrassingly.

The flare of sensuality in Keir's eyes was safely controlled by the time he reached her, but the raw note in his voice when he said, 'Put something on,' set a treacherous need preening.

Her hands shook as she accepted the bag and dragged out her floaty shirt.

When the last button was in place Keir asked without expression, 'Have you had anything to eat?'

'No. I—'

'Then you'd better have breakfast before you go home. Or

before you lie out on the beach toasting that honey-coloured skin.'

'I don't lie on the beach,' she retorted. 'I burn too easily.'

He smiled at her, his mouth suddenly relaxing into charm, pale eyes almost hypnotic in his dark face. 'Have breakfast with me, Hope,' he said softly.

That smile had always knocked the breath out of her, sent her pulse-rate into the stratosphere. 'All right,' she said before she had time to think.

Groping in her bag for a length of fine, dark green cotton gave her an excuse to avert her face in case he discerned the painful mixture of triumph and anticipatory alarm roiling in the pit of her stomach.

Keir didn't pretend not to watch as she tied the swathe of cotton over her hips, partly covering her long, bare legs. Excitement free-fell the length of her spine, dropping like a roller-coaster to explode in the pit of her stomach in a burst of fire. She took out a comb, ruthlessly slicking the wet amber mass of her hair back off her face; every cell in her body jumped, newborn and eager.

With a flick of her fingers she dropped the comb into her bag and concentrated on controlling her unruly responses.

'Now you look less likely to give the waiter a heart attack,' Keir said with a sardonic inflection that brought her head up sharply.

'This is Noosa,' she returned flippantly. 'The waiters are bullet-proof.'

'Like the shop assistants?'

'Most of us,' she said on a dry undernote of humour.

'How long have you been here?' he asked as she walked beside him along the beach. The rapidly rising sun heated her skin, cast an aureole of golden light around Keir's angular features.

'Six months or so.'

'Do you plan to stay?'

She shrugged, caution hedging her answer. 'Noosa has a lot going for it.'

Keir's brows drew together, but he asked, 'Why Australia, Hope?'

'Why not? I like it, and the people are lovely.'

'So you're just bumming along, working at jobs that don't take any of your considerable intelligence, rootless and drifting. Why are you so afraid to settle down?'

Yes, that was Keir, blunt, to the point—and high-handedly judging her. Hope thought of the travel articles that were slowly winning her a reputation, the friends she'd made—and those still waiting for her.

Cat-like, she smiled. 'What have you got against just bumming around?' she echoed, her voice deliberately lazy and amused. 'Don't knock it, Keir, if you haven't tried it.'

'I can't think of anything I'd like less. How old are you now?' His tone matched hers, its indolence somehow both sexy and intimidating, perhaps because what he said was tinged with derision.

'Don't you remember? I'm disappointed—I thought that awesomely efficient brain would have everything filed away in neat little folders. I'm twenty-three.'

'Seven years younger than I am.'

When she said nothing he glanced down at her. 'A suitable difference,' he said ambiguously.

'For what?' Hope tried to speak with matching assurance, but it was a struggle because slow anticipation burned through her, undermining the persona she'd built with such care, threatening to expose the foolish, love-sick eighteen-year-old she'd thought long buried—the girl this man had destroyed so casually, so cruelly.

Smiling, he scanned her face with deliberate, goading mockery. 'For anything,' he said. 'Would you like to eat here?'

Few people sat as yet beneath the large cream market umbrellas of the beach-front café. In an hour or so it would be buzzing.

'It has an excellent reputation,' Hope answered, clipping the words.

When a waitress tried to steer them towards a table beneath the canvas roof, Keir said, 'We'd prefer to sit over there, thank you,' nodding at one almost hidden from the rest of the patrons by potted palms.

Naturally Keir Carmichael, world-recognised billionaire, would prefer to feed shop assistants where as few people as possible could see him...

CHAPTER FOUR

STIFF-SHOULDERED, Hope sat down and pretended to read the menu. The words shimmered crazily in front of her; after a few moments she realised she was watching sunlight dance across Keir's arm, picking out a stray drop of seawater that dazzled in transparent perfection. She must have flicked it onto him.

A dark enchantment—powerful, shameless—muddied logic and reason, purring temptation through Hope's body, whispering of forbidden ecstasy. Heat coalesced in the pleasure points of her body.

Like mother, like daughter, she thought with a pang of fear; this forbidden attraction for dominant men had to be bred in the blood.

But she'd learned from her mother's tragedy. Not for her the imprisonment of love; she cherished her independence far too much to surrender it to a man who saw people as pawns. No, she'd have a liberating affair with Keir and then wave him goodbye, free at last.

She looked up into eyes of searing clarity, her breath rasping in her lungs as Keir probed her armour, searching for weak points. It took every particle of self-possession to parry that lancing, searching gaze with mildly raised eyebrows and a quizzical half-smile.

Severe mouth compressed in irony, Keir said, 'It's called desire. It exploded between us the first time I saw you, when you were eighteen and so busy hating your father you barely saw anyone else in the room. I looked at you and wanted you. And although you didn't understand it, you wanted me as much. It was mutual then, Hope; it's mutual now. But then it was impossible; it's not now.'

The warm air quivered and the sounds of the waves faded until all Hope could hear was the rapid rasp of her renewed breathing.

Reinforcing her courage with a steady voice that owed more to an arid throat than to resolution, she said crisply, 'Desire's a pretty word used by lovers. What you're talking about is closer to lust.' Or compulsion—heated, mindless and ultimately degrading.

Keir's long, measuring look attacked her defences again. 'It could grow into something more—satisfying—if we give it a chance.' His words were coolly reflective, almost thoughtful.

The soft click-click of sandals signalled a reprieve. Shrugging, Hope waited until the waitress had put down their coffee and departed before saying flatly, 'Have an affair, you mean.'

Keir avoided a direct answer. 'If that's what it takes. Finishing what we started four years ago might be good for both of us, but I'm not going to pressure you, Hope, so you can wipe that mulish look off your lovely face. I wish you'd told me what your father tried to force you to do, instead of running away.'

A cynical smile turned down the corners of her mouth. 'What would you have done?'

'Stopped it,' he said calmly.

She picked up her coffee, inhaling its delicious scent, sipping the black, aromatic brew until it steadied her. 'He was desperate enough to use whatever weapons he had, and I knew how—unreasonable he could be. It seemed sensible to remove myself from the war zone.'

'Running away is the refuge of the coward. It never solves anything,' he said, ignoring another chance to explain his actions four years previously.

'Cowardice,' Hope was stung into saying, 'is another word for self-preservation.'

'At what cost?' Keir smiled a slow challenge that set her heart pounding and dried her throat. 'Cowards never know the exhilaration of risk and adventure, of beating the odds, of winning. They live a mean, snivelling life without the joy or satisfaction of testing themselves, always skulking and looking over their shoulders.'

'Wasn't it the Chinese who said that of all the thirty-six alternatives, running away is best?' she fired back, biting out the words like small, glittering missiles. 'Once I left, my father had no leverage. He couldn't force me to do what he wanted by threatening to make my mother suffer.' Her voice still sounded barbed, so she took a swift, steadying breath.

Keir said something she was glad she didn't catch, then continued, his voice sliding into gentleness, 'What sort of childhood did you have?'

'A surprisingly stable one.' She stopped and shrugged. 'He wasn't home much. My mother loved me—in spite of everything, I always knew that. And so did her mother, my grandmother. I used to go and stay with my gran, and we had such fun together.'

Perhaps it was the violence of the emotions they'd been discussing, but she became acutely aware of a powerful, visceral response to the tang of the salt air, the warm, fecund scent of greenery and the jolt of coffee.

Looking past Keir to the beach, she watched a small boy run down to the water and dip a bucket in.

Keir said, 'I'm glad. Every child needs love. I knew right from the start that your father pushed you at me, and I knew why. I thought you were in on it—'

'I was not!'

'You were an enchanting thing, yet there was always this reserve. I wondered—perhaps it was a case of *like father, like daughter*.'

Hope's clenched hand hit the table, setting the coffee cups chattering in their saucers. 'You were totally wrong.'

'Why did your father hate you? Was it because he wanted a son?'

The small boy on the beach was now making a sandcastle with his father. Watching him, Hope said, 'He'd probably have hated a boy more—a son would have been real competition.'

Keir's black brows drew together. 'For your mother's love?'

'Exactly,' she drawled.

He leaned forward, ice-grey eyes probing, merciless. 'Let me get this right. Your father resented the fact that your mother loved you?'

'Exactly,' she repeated. Her mouth twisted into a tight, humourless smile. Holding her voice level, she went on, 'Apparently my mother used to be his secretary, and became his lover; he didn't marry her because he already had a perfectly good wife. So my mother left her job and married my birth father, who died before I was born. By then James Sanderson had divorced his first wife; he came looking for Mum and persuaded her to marry him, and then he adopted me. For the rest of her life he used me to punish her whenever she refused to obey him.'

'Obey?' Keir asked incredulously.

'That's how he thought of us,' she said. 'He owned her. He owned me. Of course, he could also use her to force me to obey him.'

Keir said something under his breath, icy eyes glittering with furious contempt.

Swallowing to moisten her dry mouth and throat, Hope muttered, 'It was a long time ago.'

'I should have stuck to my original plan and ruined him.' He spoke with a chilling lack of emotion.

The cup in Hope's hand quivered. Settling it onto the table, she asked casually, 'Why didn't you?'

He paused a moment before answering, and she looked up sharply. Was he holding something back? His harsh features revealed nothing. 'I thought he was supporting you.'

Dared she believe him? No, of course she didn't—but, oh, it was such a subtle temptation.

Crisply she said, 'Looked at from his point of view, selling me was quite a cunning plan. He probably thought it was time I paid for my board and lodging, and he wouldn't have cared if you'd broken my heart and danced on the pieces.' Hope picked up her coffee cup again and drank from it, warming herself with its heat and the quick bite of caffeine. 'I'm glad you didn't bankrupt him. He'd have found a way to blame my mother,' she said remotely.

Keir's smile showed his teeth. 'Instead I put in a receiver who traded the firm out of insolvency. Your father lost his firm, but not all his money. None of which, I gather, got to you.'

Setting the cup down with a little clatter, she said fiercely, 'I wouldn't take a cent from him. Anyway, none of that matters now.'

'If it doesn't matter, why are you still running?'

'I'm not.' Unflinchingly she met eyes the frosty clarity of a winter sky.

His lean cheeks creased into a smile—sexy as hell, an invitation to recklessness. 'So what have you been doing since you left New Zealand?'

Relieved, she told him of the six months she'd spent travelling around Great Britain and Europe with three other women in a temperamental camper-van.

He laughed at their funny, hair-raising experiences, but when she stopped he asked, 'What does Australia have that New Zealand doesn't?'

'I'm not ready to settle down.' It seemed an appropriate

time to flirt a little, show that she was responsive to his suggestion of an affair. With a swift, provocative glance from beneath her lashes, she continued, 'Strange that if your friend hadn't decided to buy herself a souvenir of Noosa you'd never have known I was living here.'

Ignoring her reference to Aline, he observed dryly, 'I'd have noticed you at the reception last night.'

Hope gave an unwilling gurgle of laughter. 'It would have been hard not to. That wretched dress—and all those diamonds!'

'Vulgar, weren't they?' he agreed. 'If your boss had any taste he'd have realised that one perfect stone—one that hinted at the warmth of your skin and hair—in a modern setting would have suited you much better than all that blue-white glitter.'

The compliment, delivered in a lazy, smoky voice, teased along her nerve-ends like a caress. When she could trust her voice to be steady, she said, 'Markus was desperate to advertise his wares, which was the reason for the dress, and to be fair it seems that it might have worked. Some people believe that you can't have too much of a good thing.'

'I'm beginning to see their point,' Keir drawled.

He had a trick of making innocuous statements reverberate with a hidden meaning. How many delicious hours had she wasted going over his conversations sentence by sentence, searching for the secret significance buried beneath the words? Too many.

'I doubt if you've ever had a lapse in taste in your whole life,' she said crisply, wishing their breakfast would arrive. She'd decided on fruit, followed by fish with an avocado salsa, while Keir had chosen fruit, too, then bacon and eggs. At least the coffee gave her something to do with her hands when he tossed those ambiguous comments at her.

Turning her head, she checked out the surroundings. The café was filling up now, with people laughing and talking and calling from table to table—Noosa on a Sunday morning, bright and brash and cheerful, with everyone determined to enjoy themselves.

One of the agreeable things about Noosa was that no one took any notice of her, even though she wore no make-up and sat with salt water drying in faint patterns on her skin, whereas every other woman in the café looked as though she'd spent at least an hour choosing delectable resort clothes and applying cosmetics.

Keir smiled. 'Of course, you know me so well,' he mocked.

Hope looked directly at him. 'I don't really know anything about you, except that we've got nothing in common.'

With narrowed eyes he surveyed her face. 'Lying to yourself is cowardly, too. What we've got in common is an extremely inconvenient response to each other. Four years hasn't dulled that appetite.' Irony lifted the corners of his mouth as he leaned over and took her hand.

With a remorseless precision that melted her bones and fired arrows of sensation through her, he kissed the fragile inner side of her wrist.

The chatter in the busy café, the laughter of the children on the beach, the soft sound of the waves—all faded into a distant hum, flat and without resonance. The only sound Hope could hear was the roaring of her blood in her ears.

Thoroughly demoralised, she blurted, 'I don't go in for casual sex.'

A smile hardened his face; his gaze rested for long, taut moments on her mouth before dropping to where the damp cotton of her shirt moulded over her breasts. Although openly sexual, that look was a stripped, stark claim, without hinting at the smutty, prying indecency of a leer.

Keir said softly, 'Neither do I. It won't be casual, Hope.'

Brazen sensation spiked through her, tightening her breasts. In spite of her clothes she felt naked, exposed, almost squirming at the clutch of desire deep inside. Only this man, she thought numbly—only Keir—had ever had this effect on her.

A man she could never allow herself to trust.

He murmured, 'I don't consider sex to be a treat, like a cold drink on a hot afternoon, a comfortable way to end the day.'

She forced herself to ignore the sensual turbulence. 'Perhaps not, but I suspect in some ways you're more like my father than you care to think.'

His lashes drooped. 'In what way?' he asked with silken aggression.

'You used my—the way I felt about you to get close to my father.'

'How? I didn't ask you questions about his firm; I didn't try to extract information about him. *He* thought of you as a bargaining tool, Hope, I didn't.' His formidable will pulled down a screen of control over the implacable features. 'I didn't even coax you into bed. Although it was bloody difficult, I behaved like a gentleman.'

The sarcasm in his voice flicked her on the raw, but before she could react a woman called out sharply, her voice rising. 'Jen! Jenny Anderson! *Come back here this minute!*'

Keir was already three steps towards the beach when he stopped, his big body relaxing. The little girl had scuttled only halfway to the water, and was already being picked up by a bystander.

The sheer, daunting speed of Keir's reflexes hit Hope like the flick of a whip. Her stomach tight with tension, she looked sideways through the screen of shrubs. It felt as though she'd been trapped at the table with him for hours.

He watched the child's mother run down and scoop her up, scolding as she carried the toddler up to another table, before he strode back, the bright, clear light dwelling on his beautifully cut mouth, the formidable line of jaw and cheek.

Hope waited until he was sitting down again before saying dryly, 'Oh, you were always a perfect gentleman.' It was amazing how skilfully he'd picked his way through the conversation without admitting his reaction to her father's offer.

But then, he was a very clever man, well seasoned in the cut-throat world of international banking; fooling a bedazzled young woman would be a doddle.

The sun shone across the black fans of his lashes, gilding the tips. Twisted by a shocking, unwelcome tenderness, Hope let her lips part slightly.

He said, 'Of course I was. You were only eighteen, young and sweet and very, very innocent.'

Keir's smile was a miracle, pure male glamour made dangerous by a dark enchantment—a heartbreaker's smile, untainted with the toothy, smug shallowness of many men who knew themselves attractive to women. It shredded the defences she'd erected with such agonising determination.

He could hurt her all over again.

But she'd survived the pain before; if she didn't take this opportunity to find out what he was like as a lover, she'd spend the rest of her life wondering and obsessing about him.

'And now,' she said smoothly, hoping he couldn't see that she was clutching her courage about her, 'I'm not so young, and definitely not so sweet or so innocent.'

Brows drawn together, Keir leaned back in his chair and surveyed her with a hint of enigmatic mockery. 'Then let's pretend we're simply old friends who've met again after some years. What good films have you seen lately?'

She knew what he was doing—gentling her—but because she wanted to eat without a churning stomach she readily told him of her reaction to the latest blockbuster, and while their food arrived, and they ate it, they spent enjoyable minutes tearing to pieces the story, the casting, the acting, and the values the movie promoted.

Too enjoyable.

From there they side-stepped to music, charting a course between her pleasure in pop and the romantic composers, and his favourites, the composers of the twenties and thirties, and the more astringent modern music.

Pulling a face, she said, 'I like a tune, not that atonal stuff. What turns you off the folk movement?'

'All the pretty idealism,' he said promptly. 'The original folk songs were earthy and practical and often cynical, honed by the centuries to purity. Apart from a few exceptions, I find modern folk music mushy.'

They'd finished eating and the plates had been removed. Hope looked up from her second cup of coffee and said wryly, 'You're not an idealist.'

'People with ideals have caused an enormous amount of damage in the world.'

He meant it, too.

Chilled, Hope said, 'That's a sweeping generalisation if ever I've heard one. A world without ideals would be a cold, soulless place. Everyone needs principles.'

'I'm not talking about them,' he said calmly. 'I have principles.'

'What's the difference?'

He lifted a devastating brow. 'A principle is an ideal with purpose and backbone.'

'It sounds good,' she agreed, 'but I'll bet that's not what the dictionary says. I'll look it up when I get home.'

'It's the definition I live by,' he said, glancing at her empty coffee cup. 'What would you like to do now? Swim again? Go for a drive? Walk?'

'I'd like to go home and shower,' she said promptly.

'And then?'

Hope dithered silently. She looked up, and met eyes that were cool and dispassionate. No pressure, he'd said; the onus was on her.

It gave her a satisfying feeling of control to know that

she'd already made the decision before he'd flung down his sexual challenge.

'We could walk in the National Park,' she suggested, keeping her voice crisp and steady. 'Have you been there?'

'No, but I'd like to.' He got to his feet and picked up her bag, reaching into his pocket as they came abreast of the till.

'Keir!'

Carefully smiling, the new owner of the goanna pin came towards them. Her veneer of poise couldn't hide the colour that winged up through her skin, or the hungry glitter in her eyes—a glitter replaced by shock when she registered Hope's presence.

'Hello, Aline,' Keir said. 'Have you met Hope Sanderson? Hope, this is Aline Connors, a colleague of mine.'

Of course the woman recognised her. Her face froze, and the hand she'd been about to thrust forward clenched, long fingers curling for a stiff moment before she gave a gracious inclination of her head. 'Hello, Hope.'

She was superbly dressed in a loose white ankle-length dress that skimmed a slim figure and hinted at good legs. A straw hat shaded her beautiful face.

Ideal resort wear. Expensive, too, in its casual subtlety.

No emotion showed in the regular features, in the large, tactfully enhanced eyes, and yet Hope felt a pang of pity. 'Hello, Ms Connors,' she said easily. 'Have you worn your pin yet?'

'Actually, no.'

Into the curt little silence Keir said smoothly, 'Hope and I are just off.'

Aline Connors's smile slipped, and was hastily retrieved. 'I just wondered what your plans are. I have a couple of e-mails I thought you might want to see, and Masterson has contacted us. He wants an answer straight away.'

'He can wait until tomorrow,' Keir told her indifferently. 'Forward the e-mails on to me.'

'I'll do that.' Another restrained smile. 'Enjoy your day.'

A very composed lady, Hope decided as they left. Those turquoise eyes hadn't once flickered across her sandy, salty clothes.

'I'll be back here in an hour,' Hope said, feeling sleazy. She was nobody's rival—she certainly had no intention of fighting a battle over this man. She met Keir's ironic, questioning glance square-on, giving nothing away.

'Don't you want me to find out where you live?' he asked cynically.

'I don't like being used to warn off an encumbrance.'

They'd reached the discreet entrance to Noosa's most expensive and exclusive apartment block. Stopping, Keir returned curtly, 'Eighteen months ago Aline's husband—a friend—was killed in an accident. They'd been very happy together. For some reason she's persuaded herself that she's in love with me. I value her as a colleague and I care for her as my friend's widow. Eventually she'll get over it, and in the meantime I can deal with the situation—I don't need to drag anyone else into it.'

He finished in an uncompromising tone, 'This has nothing to do with Aline.' And he bent his head and kissed the spot where Hope's neck met her shoulder.

His lips were cool and gentle, and then they were hot and hard, and at their touch desire burned like an unstoppable blast of lightning, fierce, potent, as searing as the icy fire of his eyes.

It wasn't enough, Hope thought dazedly.

Keir imprisoned her hand against his chest, so that she could feel his heart driving into the palm, a jagged counterpoint to the oppressive desire that shuddered through her.

A hair's breadth from her skin, he said implacably, 'This is between you and me, Hope; no one else has any part in it.' Each word, each unbidden almost-kiss, battered at the foundations of her control.

'No,' she breathed, horrified because the hunger inside her demanded instant satisfaction. Instinct drove her to pull away.

For a moment his hand clamped on hers; their eyes locked, frost duelling with flame, but before she had time to utter the protest on her lips he let her go and took a step back.

'You're free,' he said with a detachment belied by the glitter in his eyes, the raw note in his voice. 'Free to go wherever and whenever you like.'

'I thought—but I don't want this,' she said unsteadily, her driving purpose forgotten in a blast of primitive alarm.

'Do you think *I* do?'

'I didn't know…' The words trailed away into silence.

Keir didn't touch her. He gave her no easy excuse, exerted no calculated fascination, so that she couldn't ever look back and say, It wasn't my fault, he persuaded me into it. He simply watched her with those glacial eyes.

Thoughts tumbling endlessly, Hope felt the imprint of his kisses on her skin as though he'd branded her, claimed her in a primal way beyond the reach of reason.

'You're free to do whatever you want,' he said with biting clarity. 'But always remember that you were the coward, the one who ran.'

Her eyes roamed the slashing, strong angles and planes of his face, the ruthless jaw and chin, the black brows and lashes. Just once, she thought with a swift rebellious flare, she'd like to know real passion, real desire—yes, even real lust.

If she dared, she'd experience something potent and primal—a relationship with no commitment, no strings, no unbearable emotional claims; a relationship that was true and untrammelled because both she and Keir understood that there'd be nothing more to it than the satisfaction of a need, the sating of frustration left to seethe unsuspected for too long.

Reckless hunger uncoiled inside her, insistent, demanding, twisting through her body, pulling urgently at her.

'Well, Hope?' Keir's voice shattered the thick, seductive silence.

Swallowing, she said, 'I can walk away,' because it was important he understand this.

He nodded, an enigmatic smile curling his hard mouth.

She finished, 'But I choose not to.'

Something kindled in the pale eyes. 'I understand,' Keir said, his voice deep and a little harsh. 'I'll get the car keys and drive you home.' He took her arm and turned her towards the entrance of the apartments.

Head spinning, because she'd just agreed to an affair with Keir Carmichael, Hope walked beside him into the foyer, all glass and marble and manicured foliage. A waterfall splashed discreetly from the wall into a pool adorned by a sculpted bronze waterlily leaf, on which basked a large frog, also bronze.

Clad in a damp shirt and sarong, neither of which had been elegant to begin with, Hope felt distinctly out of place, especially when a woman whose smart suit appeared to have been sprayed onto her approached them. 'I have a message for you, Mr Carmichael,' she said, carefully not looking at Hope. 'It's marked "urgent".'

Frowning, he said, 'Thank you.' He turned to Hope.

Before he could speak she said quickly, 'I'll wait here,' and walked across to the edge of the waterfall. To the sound of its soothing murmur she admired the talent it must have taken to set up this calm oasis.

Although she'd grown up shielded from poverty, the past few years had shown her another side of life. There was nothing, she thought cynically, like being poor to change your outlook. Why hadn't all this money and talent been used to help people who were desperate for the basics of life?

Not that it was as simple as a straight transferral of money from one pocket to another. Nothing in this life was ever simple. And now she was doing what she'd always vowed she'd never do: waiting around until some man had time for her.

The bravado that had driven her decision to take Keir for a lover ebbed away, leaving her as bewildered as a fish stranded in a rock pool. Panic compelled her to her feet, but before she had time to take more than two steps towards the doors, a woman came through them, a woman whose face set into rigid lines when she saw Hope.

'Are you waiting for Keir? He shouldn't be long,' Aline Connor said with odious, patronising sympathy. 'Shall we go and sit down over there? It's well done, this foyer, isn't it? It strikes just the right note for a place like Noosa—light-hearted yet luxurious. Have you been here before?'

Leading the way, she headed towards a group of chairs and sat down in one, clearly expecting Hope to do the same. Unable to get away without looking a total idiot, Hope joined her.

'No,' she said evenly. 'I haven't.'

Aline Connors gave her a swift look. 'You're very beautiful,' she commented.

'Thank you,' Hope murmured, uneasy now.

The older woman said unexpectedly, 'I'd probably like you if we got to know each other. You remind me a bit of someone very dear to me. She had that sort of golden luxuriance about her, too—a warm richness that reminds me of an Earth Mother.' She gave a little laugh with no humour in it. 'You can treat this as the warning of a jealous woman if you like, because to some extent it is. However, I think you should know that Keir doesn't want commitment.'

Firmly repressing the urge to inform her that commitment was the last thing she wanted from Keir, Hope said, 'I don't think you should be discussing him with me.'

'He's been chased all his life,' Aline Connors said thoughtfully. 'He's always been extremely attractive to women—and of course his power and money make him even more of a target. Our sex can be utterly ruthless. He doesn't trust women.'

Hope kept silent.

After a moment Aline resumed, 'Eventually he'll want to marry, and he'll choose someone who won't demand intense emotions from him.'

With a stark flash of insight, Hope realised that because Aline had already loved with all-consuming desperation she didn't expect it to happen again. So she'd made a lifestyle choice and planned to take what she believed were the only things Keir could give her—money, children and an assured position.

'Why are you telling me this?' Hope asked quietly.

Aline Connors surveyed her nails—short, practical, discreet, yet immaculately presented. 'To warn you off,' she admitted, looking up with a sympathetic smile. 'If all you want is a fling, then he's brilliant in bed and generous and thoughtful—perfect. But if you want any more, you're going to be very unhappy.'

I *don't* believe he's made love with you, Hope thought, revolted and angry—then wondered whether she was being naïve again. Aline was entirely confident; she saw Hope as no threat to her plans, nothing but a pretty bimbo who could be dismissed in this offhand way.

She and Keir deserved each other.

The older woman's eyes went past Hope; her face smoothed into a warm smile and she got gracefully to her feet. 'Ah, there you are, Keir. I've been keeping Hope company.'

'Thank you,' he said crisply, his glance resting for a disturbing second on Hope's face.

CHAPTER FIVE

KEIR waited until they were in his anonymous rental car, and Hope had told him which road to take, before asking, 'What did Aline have to say?'

'She was just being friendly.' Whatever suspicions Hope might have about the other woman's integrity, she couldn't see any point in revealing them, so she concentrated on directing Keir.

'Here?' he said, pulling into the driveway beside the leafless branches of the frangipani.

'Yes. I won't be long.' Hurriedly she asked, 'Did you bring a hat? Sunscreen?'

'Both,' he said blandly.

Because it seemed rude to leave him in the car, she said, 'I'd ask you in, only it's just one room.'

His mouth tightened. 'I'll wait here.'

Ten minutes later she walked sedately through the door, absurdly concerned to see an empty car. A glance along the street revealed Keir talking to the two children and the dog from next door.

'Hello,' she said as she approached. 'Hi, Jaedan, Abby, Butch.'

'Hi, Hope,' the children chorused, grinning as widely as the dog.

'Hope,' Keir said, his eyes amused, 'why didn't you tell me you're a demon bowler?'

'Only in this neighbourhood,' she told him, patting the head of the black and white border collie. 'Have you kids been telling tales out of school?'

'Can't see any school around,' Jaedan said cheerfully, 'so we musta been. You gunna play cricket for us today?'

'Not this morning; we're going out,' Hope said.

'We're not playing until after lunch.' Jaedan pulled a hideous face. 'If you don't come they're gunna slaughter us.'

'Our cousins and uncle and auntie from Bundaberg are here,' Abby informed her gloomily, 'and they're good. Mum's the best, but you know Dad, he's got butterfingers, and although Butch tries hard he runs away with the ball.' She eyed Keir up. 'Can you catch?'

'Reasonably well,' he said, adding, 'I'm quite a good batsman.'

'Then you come, too,' Jaedan instructed with the eagerness of someone who sees salvation on the horizon. 'Ab, we'd better go.'

Abby looked at Keir. 'Thank you for grabbing Butch. He goes crackers when he sees magpies—just won't listen. I thought he might get run over again. Last time it cost about a thousand dollars to fix him up, and Dad said if he did it again Butch'd have to earn the money for the vet. But a dog can't work.'

'You could try aversion therapy,' Keir suggested, looking down at the dog, all panting eagerness and wagging tail. 'Squirt him with a water pistol whenever he does anything you don't like. A friend of mine did that with a Boxer that chased cars, and it worked. You'll probably find a book on dog training in the library, or you could talk to the vet.'

'Yeah,' Abbey said thoughtfully.

Back in the car Keir said, 'Nice kids.'

'They're great kids.' He'd been good with them, not treating them like another species the way some adults did. When he finally settled to his miserable, emotionless marriage with Aline, or someone like her, he'd make a good father.

*　　*　　*

'When Australians get nostalgic overseas, they burn eucalyptus leaves and cry into their beer,' Hope said, stepping back to admire the smoothly marbled trunk of one of the big gum trees in the National Park. Sunlight poured amber through the sparse canopy of leaves and over the grey-green and gold and silvery tan of the bark.

'Do you long for our bush?' Keir asked lazily in his deep, even voice with its tantalising undercurrent of sensuality. Sitting on the ground—long legs stretched out in front of him, back against the tree, face shadowed by the brim of his hat—he was as relaxed and graceful as a tiger after a kill.

Pacing across to the edge of the cliff, she frowned over the fence at the waves purring against the rock ledges below.

'I do miss it,' she admitted. 'It's so different from this dry eucalyptus woodland.' Anchoring her gaze to the tracery of foam against the rocks, she went on, 'When I was five or six we visited a kauri forest in Northland. It was summer, but a huge thunderhead was building in the sky and the air was very still. You know that odd green light you get when it's going to thunder, and the heavy silence?'

'Yes.'

'I had a friend with me and we ran down the tracks yelling and laughing and whooping like banshees. Our voices echoed and rang through those enormous trees that waited and watched and weighed us down with their presence. I remember what it smelt like—rich and damp and mysterious.'

'Not an entirely happy recollection.' Opaque as molten silver, his eyes successfully hid his thoughts.

A dizzying vortex of sensation robbed Hope of words, of thought, flinging her into a space where all she could experience was the oppressive heat, and the tangy scent of the gums, and Keir's unsettling scrutiny.

Wrenching her gaze away, she said thickly, 'Not entirely.'

'Your father?'

He was too astute. 'He didn't say anything, but Mum and

I knew he was angry—we could read the signs. He waited until my friend was dropped off and then he went ballistic because I was so undisciplined. When we got home he made Mum give me a hiding.' Her hand stole up to the little scar on her chin, then dropped away.

Keir said between his teeth, 'He's a psychopath.'

She didn't hear him get up, but her skin announced his arrival and without resistance she leaned into his embrace, taking a complicated comfort from his power and his strength.

'Did your father abuse you?' Keir asked in a swift, lethal voice that dried her mouth. 'Is that why you won't go home?'

'He never lifted a hand to me.'

After a moment's silence he said harshly, 'There are other types of abuse.'

Heat from his body enveloped her, and to her astonishment she realised she felt secure. 'He didn't sexually or physically abuse me.'

'What about that scar?'

She hesitated, then admitted, 'My mother's engagement ring caught my skin. It was barely a scratch.'

'So he emotionally abused you both.' The silky undernote in his voice gave the words a deadly inflection. 'I wouldn't wish dementia on my worst enemy, but it seems almost a just retribution that he's now in the secure wing of a hospital, immobilised with it.'

Horrified, she shuddered, but a weight she'd never suspected eased from her. 'I didn't know,' she muttered.

Keir said, 'It's bitterly ironic that the money he wanted so much is being used to pay for his nursing. Come and sit down.'

It was too easy to accept his comfort, and comfort was not what she wanted from him. Keeping her face averted, she sat a careful distance away, fixing her eyes on the limitless, glowing blue of the Coral Sea in front. Insects, tiny gleaming bullets in the shimmering air, hummed and buzzed around them. A bird of prey soared above, head and breast radiantly white in the sun as it tilted and manoeuvred on the air currents before swooping with lethal speed on some small animal or bird in the bushland behind them.

'What is it?' Keir asked, following her gaze.

'A brahminy kite,' she told him. 'They're quite common.'

'Do they frighten you? You shivered.'

'No. I was thinking of my father.' She paused before finishing brightly, 'I'm terrified of snakes. And I don't like spiders much. Unfortunately Australia has a good quota of both.'

Ice-coloured eyes searched hers, piercing, almost hypnotic, probing for something she wasn't prepared to yield. Quickly, before he found it, she hid behind her lashes.

'Hope,' he said quietly.

With one sense blocked the others were much more acute, yet she heard nothing, felt nothing, until his arms came around her again.

Still hiding behind her lashes, she lifted her face in silent invitation.

This time he didn't offer comfort. His mouth was hard and consuming; he kissed her like a conqueror, and he tasted like danger—an edged danger that mingled with the flavours of desire and passion—like everything her untried body and heart had sought without knowing all through the years.

Hope forgot the rest of the world in the keen delight of his mouth and the singing hunger that soared up from some well-spring inside her. By the time the kiss ended she'd have followed him across the world. Blindly, mutely, she turned her face into his throat, ensnared by the heavy thudding of his heart as she fought for control.

'All right?' he murmured into her hair.

For a last, precious moment she lay against him, then pulled away, opening her eyes to stare sightlessly across to the dazzling ultramarine of the horizon.

'I'm fine,' she said brusquely, getting to her feet and smoothing her hair back from her face with shaking, uncertain hands as she walked towards the railing above the cliff.

This incandescent physical attraction was even more shattering than it had been when she was eighteen. Repressed and slumbering, it had been four years proving. If she gave in to it she could end up addicted.

It wasn't too late to call a halt. Bending to pick up a dry twig and throw it into the sea, she watched the small stick fall, lifting in the breeze now and then, until it landed on the flat rocks at the base. A wave came over and when it sucked back the rock ledge was empty.

She could still walk away without any serious damage done.

If she was a coward.

Keir had been watching her, his eyes hooded and speculative, but when she straightened up he was on his feet, tiger-striped by the sun through the leaves. 'If it's any consolation,' he said drily, 'it hasn't happened like that to me again, either.'

'It is some sort of consolation,' she admitted with gritty frustration, 'but I resent the—the *mindlessness* of it.' She thumped a furious hand on the railing. 'What is it, anyway?'

It was just a rhetorical question, a way to use up some of the adrenalin that seethed through her, but Keir laughed quietly, almost grimly, and said, 'Most scientists seem to feel it's to do with the balance of chemicals in the brain.'

'Oh, *really*!' Anger, quick and cathartic, flagged her skin. 'I resent that, too. I'm more than just a collection of hormones and chemicals. And even if it's true, what sets them off?'

'Who knows?' His mouth crooked in a smile that held something of amusement but more of irony, he caught her hand and lifted it to his mouth.

Hope froze, her whole being focused on the place where

his lips met her palm, concentrating so intently that the only sounds she heard were the unsteady thunder of her heart and her quick, ragged inhalation when his tongue traced across her sensitive skin. Tendrils of need uncurled from the skin under his mouth and wound through her, tightening in her breasts before diving down to the point between her thighs where passion flowered. She wanted to arch her body against his, she wanted to stretch beneath him and take from him the strength and heat of his body—she wanted everything...

'That's your heartline,' he said softly against her hand. 'And this is your lifeline. You're shaking, Hope.'

'I know,' she said raggedly.

'I never forgot you. You still take up far too much room in my mind.' He stopped and stared at her, pale eyes glittering in his tanned face. 'And you didn't forget me.'

Sweat trickled down Hope's back, gathered in beads across her temples. Somewhere close by a bird screamed, the harsh sound closely followed by a liquid melody she barely heard; both calls were blocked by Keir's words—brusque, emphatic, angry—tumbling inside her head.

'I didn't forget you,' she whispered, and knew there'd be no turning back now. The reckless violence of her response convinced her that she had to surrender, sate herself in what he offered before she could at last leave him behind. Forbidden excitement stirred her senses, sang through her veins, spurred on her responses. She should be exultant, but it was terror that gripped her.

No, not terror—just fear of the unknown. She had nothing to lose.

'Someone's coming. Let's go,' Keir said on a raw note, turning away.

He'd taken three strides along the path before Hope realised that he wasn't going to wait for her to reassemble her shattered poise. Swallowing, she dragged in a couple of shallow breaths before setting off after him.

Keir glanced over his shoulder and slowed.

'I'm right behind you,' she said, and immediately wished she hadn't spoken, because her emotions ran in a husky current beneath the words.

A group of people strolled towards them, laughing, calling out. Keir took Hope's elbow and eased her to one side so they could pass, then released her.

'There's a colony of koalas in these trees,' she remarked when she could once more trust her voice. For the next ten minutes she pointed out anything she thought might be of interest to him, and quite a lot that probably wasn't.

It gave her time to recover, although she caught sardonic comprehension in his eyes when she indicated Double Island Point far to the north and informed him that it was a volcanic headland responsible for anchoring the splendid northwards sweep of Cooloola Beach and Rainbow Beach.

'Have you seen the coloured sand cliffs?' she asked chattily.

'No.'

'Oh, you should! They're very impressive. And Sunshine Beach—'

'Hope, we're both New Zealanders,' he said mockingly. 'Why would we go to see beaches? We have enough of our own.'

'Then you must go up Lake Cootheraba,' she hurried on. 'It's a great trip. The water in the river is so heavily stained with tannin that the reflections are wonderful.'

He said crisply, 'I plan to see the lakes one day.'

A sneaked glance at his face revealed nothing but a relaxed interest in the bush and the scenery; he began to ask about birds they heard, and Hope tried to answer as though that kiss had never happened.

Perhaps to him it meant nothing.

No, she thought, he couldn't hide his response; to him that

kiss signified the same limiting, inconvenient obsession that had never died in her.

Eventually they arrived at Alexandria Bay, and strolled along the sand, looking south along the white arc of Sunshine Beach.

They decided to go back over the hill instead of repeating their outward path, and were halfway there in the rapidly heating sun when Keir suddenly grasped her arm to bring her up short, and in a continuation of the swift movement pushed her behind him.

'What—?' she demanded, peering around his broad back.

'I saw something—' His voice cut off. After a second he laughed quietly. 'I thought they stayed in the trees.'

'What?' She peered past him. A small, dusty-looking koala was shambling towards them, its fur dull, its eyes blinking in the sun, its teddy-bear charm worn shabby. Uncertainly Hope said, 'I don't think they come out in the daytime, and they certainly don't usually come up to people.'

'It's sick, then.'

'It must be. Oh, look, look—it's stumbling, poor thing.'

Pathetically, the koala fell, hunching on the dusty ground. Hope started towards it, to be prevented by a ruthless hand around her wrist.

'Don't touch it,' Keir commanded. 'I'll ring for help. The rangers will know how to deal with it.'

He took out his cellphone, and within seconds was talking crisply. 'Exactly where are we?' he asked Hope, handing over the phone so she could explain.

When she gave it back to him he said, 'We'll stay until you get here,' he said. 'No, we won't go near it.'

In a surprisingly short time a uniformed ranger arrived, congratulated them on leaving the animal alone, and within seconds had it safely secured.

'It's probably some infection,' he said. 'I'll get it to the vet. Thanks, both of you, you've given it a chance.'

His smile at Hope conveyed appreciation of her legs and the respect a man gives to the alpha male's partner. Gritting her teeth, she smiled back.

Mockery glimmered in Keir's eyes, curved the corners of his mouth.

'For a moment,' he said in a dry voice when the ranger had left them with his precious bundle, 'I wondered whether he was going to scoop you up and take you away instead of the koala.'

'I hope the koala is all right,' she said, taming the snap in her tone.

'I hope so, too.'

Curiosity made her ask, 'What's your favourite animal?'

'Cats,' he said. 'I like their independence and their single-minded determination to get their own way. What's yours?'

'Cats, too.'

He smiled at her, and her heart flipped. 'So we have that in common,' he said quite gently. 'And we'd better get going; it might be what passes for winter here but the sun's hot.'

Back at her place, he switched off the engine, but before he could speak the Petrie children appeared at the end of the drive, fizzing with eagerness.

Abby announced importantly, 'Mum says come for lunch, Hope. We're having a barbecue, and she said if the man wants to come, too, he can, 'cos we need all the help we can get.'

Australians were famed for their hospitality, and never more so than to strangers; at that precise moment Hope considered it a vastly overrated quality.

Val Petrie, the children's mother, arrived behind them. 'I didn't put it exactly like that,' she said to her offspring, and directed a smile at Hope. When she transferred it to Keir, the older woman's gaze widened in involuntary tribute to his uncompromising masculinity.

After the introductions Val said, 'Keir, we'd like it very much if you'd come for lunch, too. And, in spite of my sports-mad kids, it's not because you're a good batsman, although this is the equivalent of a test match.'

Keir's charged charm blazed forth in his smile, further dilating Val's eyes. 'I'd like it very much,' he said. 'What time does this test match start?'

'The men have just come in from fishing, so we'll eat some fish and the prawns with salad, and then get going. Come up now, if you like.' Val's eyes gleamed with laughter. 'It's always nice meeting Hope's friends, especially when they play a good game of cricket.'

Keir's mouth tightened, but his voice was smooth and amused. 'I'm making no promises,' he said.

At ten o'clock that night Hope and Keir walked down the Petries' driveway and along the short stretch of footpath to his car. The exotic, disturbing musk of jasmine flowers floated in the sultry air, mingling with the faint, ever-present tang of eucalyptus.

'Did you enjoy the evening?' Hope asked.

When Val had suggested they stay for dinner Keir had lifted his brows at Hope, and at her nod had agreed.

He said now, 'Very. They're a pleasant bunch. It would have been nice if we'd beaten the team from Bundaberg, though.'

'Competitive to the end,' she said, smiling.

'That's me.' His voice was level.

In spite of the best efforts of the home side, the hard-fought test match had been won by the visitors. Afterwards the men had turned sausages and chicken and more delicious fish on the barbecue, to the tune of excited laughter and shrieks from the pool. They'd talked about fishing and football and politics and whether *haute couture* was serious or just a big con job, and whether New Zealand would ever become an Australian state.

A typical Sunday night, completely transformed by Keir's presence. Hope had wondered whether he might not feel out of place, but she should have known better. He hadn't courted popularity, yet within minutes he'd fitted in. Men, she knew, were acutely conscious of status, and they'd taken one look at Keir and accepted him as worthy of respect.

And the women had looked at him with open appreciation that marked his height and his wide shoulders and long legs, his lithe male stance, and the vital essence of masculinity that radiated from him like a dark flame.

As for the children—well, his prowess with the bat had reduced the boys to hero-worship, and he'd been targeted by one three-year-old girl who'd flirted shyly with him for the first part of the evening and spent the second half in his arms, sound asleep.

All in all, he'd been a resounding success and charmed the pants off her friends.

Hope wondered why she was so irritated.

'What was the weather like when you left Auckland?' she asked too abruptly, breaking into a silence that had assumed a prickly significance.

'Wet. Cold.' His expression told her he knew what she was doing, but he went on, 'It's hard to believe it's winter here.'

It still amused her when the locals shrugged into jerseys and sweatshirts. 'Queenslanders would die in a typical southerly. Mind you, so would I now.'

Although they weren't touching, his closeness echoed through every singing cell in her. If this, she thought mordantly, was a mere chemical reaction, it was a miracle someone hadn't found out how to bottle it. They'd make their fortune. She felt truly alive—alive and aware, and eager for something she'd never experienced.

It was a dangerous sensation, one she had to control.

Swallowing, she said in a bright, unconvincing tone, 'I used to envy kids who could laugh with their parents. Is that the sort of family evening you had when you were a boy?'

He stopped by his car and looked down at her, his mouth twisting in his dark face, his eyes half closed. 'Something like that,' he murmured. 'I had a very ordinary, standard childhood. My parents loved me; my mother was the classic stay-at-home who spoiled me and my father always had time for me. I grew up, worked hard, and here I am.' His voice altered, deepened. 'And here you are.'

He turned her gently into his arms and looked down into her face. The erotic scent of the jasmine lapped around them, filling her head with fumes, but it was Keir's touch that transformed the tension she'd been suffering all evening into a lazy, drugged hunger.

'You're so beautiful,' he said, his voice harsh. 'Glowing and golden—a summer woman, with summery eyes and a husky summery voice, and a laugh like liquid sunshine.'

Yet he didn't kiss her—or not where she wanted him to. Instead of the fiery passion Hope expected—craved—his mouth touched her forehead gently.

'You even smell of summer,' he murmured. 'Sunshine, jasmine and just a hint of barbecue...' He kissed her temples, and the soft lines of her lashes, and the tip of her nose.

Charmed, lulled, mesmerised, she lifted her seeking face. His mouth settled briefly on one corner of hers, traced the outline in a series of light kisses that left her increasingly hungry.

Astonished and embarrassed, Hope heard herself make a sound in her throat, half-growl, half-purr. She felt his smile against her skin, then that tormenting, tantalising mouth found the edge of her jaw under her ear, and he nipped the satin skin there.

It didn't hurt, but shock jerked her backwards. Not far,

however, for his arms contracted and she was pulled into the vital strength of his big, aroused body, held there while his possessive mouth took her famished kiss and returned it.

Locked together, they kissed in the friendly darkness until Hope could no longer think, until all she could feel was a vast, compelling urgency that rode her with fearsome insistence, more necessary to her than her own breath.

The noise of a car missing a gear on the hill finally broke into the swirling, heated cocoon of desire that enclosed them. She breathed Keir's name into his skin, and wondered at the blurry, disconnected sound of her own voice.

He said in harsh, impeded tones, 'I'll walk you to your door.'

'Yes,' she said thinly, and went with him into the yard and along the path to her door.

'Sleep well,' he said, waiting until she was inside with the door safely locked between them before striding back to the car.

Disappointment sawed through her. Standing well back from the windows, she watched him through the screen, every cell in her body tortured with frustration. How could he shut down that intense, demanding passion so abruptly?

Easily. Four years previously he'd kissed her and excited her, courted her and made her feel beautiful—and then, night after night, week after week, month after month, taken her home.

The headlights flashed a moment; she shielded her face with her hand, hoping he hadn't seen her through the window. Striving to tamp down the seething hunger that prowled through her, she listened as the hired car purred slowly away.

Only when she could hear nothing more did she turn and walk into the tiny bathroom.

A vicious twist of her fingers took the cap off the bottle of cleanser. Almost shivering, she patted the liquid over her hot face.

Four years ago she'd been little more than a schoolgirl. Her friends had spent their evenings fighting off their boyfriends, but Keir had treated her with a leashed courtesy she'd innocently taken to be respect.

God, she'd been such a baby!

She wiped her face and stared unseeingly at her reflection. Had she missed an opportunity tonight? If she'd asked him in, would he have come?

'But you didn't ask him,' she told her reflection irritably. 'And why are you talking to yourself in the mirror? Perhaps you should get a cat.'

She pulled a face and stripped, tossing her clothes into the basket. Uneasy, still possessed by a raging need, she showered, turning the cold tap onto full and letting the water play over her until she began to shiver.

The seesaw of decision-making flung her earthwards again. The sensible thing to do would be to refuse Keir's invitations, make sure she never saw him again.

Yet that traitorous hunger played devil's advocate. Almost wrecking her wrist with a savage jerk on the shower controls, she stepped out and began to rub herself dry.

She didn't *want* to be sensible. She wanted to experience what Keir offered, the hazardous—and temporary—promise of sexual fulfilment.

And freedom, she reminded herself, from this feverish need.

'Oh, why not say it? You want Keir Carmichael,' she said aloud. 'You lust after him, you eat him with your eyes, you want to go to bed with him, you want to know what it's like to feel him inside you. You're completely hung up on the man, and you have been ever since you met him.'

Ever since he smiled at you at your first grown-up party, a prim inner voice scoffed.

Her vigorous towel strokes slowed, stopped, as flames licked through her skin, through secret inner pathways, through every sinew, every cell—a heat that carried the seeds of its satiation.

She wanted him so much she *ached* with it.

Was this how her mother had felt about her father—this physical compulsion to give and give and take and take?

Shivering, she finished drying herself off. Yes, she had only to think of her mother to quench the sudden charge that fired her blood.

But when she'd pulled out her diary she stared blindly at the heavy notebook and wondered whether she was crazy for hoping that an affair with Keir would finally set her free of this dark obsession.

Gritting her teeth, she began to write, only stopping an hour later when she realised that she'd strayed into fiction, and that the scene unfolding beneath her racing fingers was so incendiary it almost smoked off the page.

'I *must* be going mad,' she muttered, slamming the book shut. Erotic fantasies, for heaven's sake! Although her travel articles found a ready market, she'd never written fiction before, or wanted to.

What was Keir doing to her?

She flung herself into bed, yanked the sheet up and folded angry arms behind her head, glowering at the ceiling.

If I'd just been a little more forward, I might be making love with him now, she thought wildly, imagining Keir standing beside the bed, looking down at her, his wide shoulders bare...

Her stomach clamped and she sat up and switched the light on to stare around the room. Her lips twitched.

This was hardly a room to seduce a man in—clean and comfortable though it was, the single bed wouldn't hold Keir by himself, let alone the two of them. And the place was basic, to say the least. The only things paying lip service to the electronic age were her small television set and CD player, and the geriatric laptop she needed to replace before it finally died.

Sighing, she switched off the light, turned over and punched a pillow. Even if she transformed her room into a haven of sensuous sin, there was her nice, elderly landlady, sleeping lightly on the floor above.

Besides, she had no seductive nightwear, and she didn't know who provided the condoms in an encounter such as she'd fantasised.

She also didn't have the faintest idea how you went about seducing a man.

It didn't matter, she thought defiantly; she'd learn.

She drifted into sleep, where in several different dreams she had no trouble at all seducing Keir.

CHAPTER SIX

BOUNCING out of the office as Hope walked into the shop on Monday, Markus said in a significant voice, 'I think we've sold that necklace.'

'Good,' Hope returned. 'Anyone we know—a film star, perhaps?'

His mouth turning down, he tapped the side of his nose. 'He wants discretion.'

Five minutes later the smile had vanished entirely. He drove a stubby finger at the letter Hope had just given him and asked sharply, 'What does this mean?'

'What it says,' Hope said, a little startled. 'I'll be moving on in a couple of weeks.'

'Why?' He stared at her as though she'd taken leave of her senses. 'If it's a question of money—'

'It's not,' she interrupted briskly.

He made a petulant face. 'Wanderlust, that's your problem. I shouldn't have offered you a commission.'

She laughed. 'Don't blame the commission. I've been in Noosa longer than I normally stay anywhere.'

'I don't understand you young things,' he said, shaking his head. 'Or perhaps I'm just envious. Where are you heading for? Back to New Zealand?'

She shrugged. 'I have a hankering to go inland. I've seen coastal Australia, but not the Outback.'

'Dust and flies and snakes and heat,' he said, ruthlessly dismissing most of his native land. 'You'll hate it.'

Hiding a smile, Hope went to the front of the shop, where she sold three small gold charms—a kangaroo, emu and koala—to a harassed man who confided that they were for his daughters. For his wife he chose a necklace of sterling silver and pearls, an especially handsome piece made by a local artisan.

As she handed him his credit card slip, Hope found herself wondering what it would be like to be able to spend that amount of money without even thinking about it.

She busied herself tidying the contents of the cases, carefully rearranging the beautiful, expensive results of humanity's obsession with adornment and prestige. Had Keir been right? Was she just drifting?

Even her writing was a part-time thing…

Several minutes later her skin tightened, pulling upright the tiny hairs across the nape of her neck. She glanced across sharply to see Keir walk in through the door.

'Good morning,' he said, teasing her a little. 'Did you sleep well?'

'Of course,' she lied, closing the case and locking it.

'I didn't.' His gaze swept her face with something dangerously close to possessiveness, but when her eyes met his he frowned, and splinters of ice collected in the translucent grey depths, dispelling the heat. 'What's the matter?'

She couldn't tell him that possessiveness brought old fears jangling to the surface. 'Nothing.'

Although her answer didn't satisfy him, a customer's arrival meant that he had to content himself with a nod that promised further discussion. 'I might be a little late tonight; if so, I'll ring.' His hooded eyes scanned her face as though searching for something.

'All right.'

Hope knew the moment he'd left because her pulses settled down to normal, although anticipation still hummed languorously through her.

The day turned hot and steamy. By mid-morning people began to drift inside in a search for air-conditioning; although they looked most didn't buy, contenting themselves with trying things on and complaining about the unseasonable heat and humidity.

Hope got tired of murmuring soothingly, 'There'll probably be a thunderstorm later in the afternoon. That will clear the air.'

Sure enough, just after she'd set off into the stifling humidity, she heard the first low rumble and looked up to see a black band of cloud ominously working its way up from the south. Sweat gathered at her temples, trickled unpleasantly down her spine, and she couldn't breathe in the heavy, hot air.

When a car drew up beside her she didn't turn until she heard Keir's voice saying, 'Get in, Hope. It's going to rain.'

'Not yet,' she said, climbing in.

'I thought of taking you on a picnic,' he said, setting the car in motion again, 'but it's clearly not a good idea. We'll go to Philibert's.'

'The restaurant with the temperamental owner who never lets more than four people—four exclusive, incredibly rich and powerful people—at a time into his dining room?'

His mouth quirked. 'That's the place.'

'The restaurant famous for its ambrosial food and its huge and eclectic wine list?'

'The same one.'

She looked at him with pity. 'I'd adore to go, but you have to book at least a month ahead.'

'It's all right,' he told her, 'I've reserved a table.'

Well, of course. What chef—however temperamental—was going to turn Keir Carmichael down?

'How wonderful,' she said, and added slyly, 'If only I'd known earlier. Markus would probably have offered to borrow something from his wife's salon for me to wear and pressed jewellery on me—as long as I promised to mention both shops loudly at least ten times, of course.'

Keir lifted an eyebrow. 'And would you have taken up his offer?'

'Once was more than enough—I felt like a prize heifer in a show ring.'

'Staked and surrounded by wolves,' Keir said shortly. 'But you kept your dignity.'

The memory of that moment when Keir had looked at Harry Forsayth with flat, deadly eyes jangled already overstretched nerves. Hope licked dry lips and said, 'Markus has been good to me, and he was desperate to sell the necklace.'

'Then he should have got his wife or daughter to wear it,' Keir said austerely.

'He had a bet on with his wife, and be fair, Keir, he organised a bodyguard as well as keeping an eye on me himself.' It seemed a good idea to change the subject. 'Tell me, what should I wear to a place like Philibert's?'

'Whatever you want to. You always look superb.'

The compliment was delivered in a cool, impersonal voice. Did he think she was fishing? Cordially she said, 'Well, thank you. So do you.'

Eyes glinting, he said, 'I meant it.'

'So did I.'

He laughed softly and turned into her street. 'All right, next time I'll inject more enthusiasm into my voice.'

'Don't bother injecting,' she said calmly. 'If your tone doesn't match your words you always run the risk of being disbelieved.'

'You've grown into a very frank woman.'

'You should have remembered that subtlety is not my strong suit.' She'd watched her father's vicious subtlety wreck her mother's life.

The muttering cloud alerted her senses; it hung over them, intensifying the light into a lurid green, weighing them down with its darkness. Carefully Hope loosened her hands in her lap, relaxed the small muscles of her face.

'I'll pick you up in a couple of hours. I assume it will be cooler after the rain,' Keir said as he drove into the driveway.

'Yes, and fresher—much less humid.'

Lightning flashed inside the cloud; when she flinched, Keir asked, 'Are you afraid of thunderstorms?'

'Not really.' She scrabbled at the handle, finally jerking the door open. 'It's going to rain like hell in a few minutes, so you'd better get under cover before it comes.'

Without giving him a chance to answer, she slammed the door behind her and ran for the house. Once in its shelter she stiffened her shoulders, pasted on a smile and turned to wave, but Keir was only two steps behind her, his face set in fierce, predatory lines.

Another bolt of lightning pinned her in its livid glare. Witless, unable to think, she gulped air into starved lungs and stared at him with painfully wide eyes. 'Don't worry, Keir.' She renewed the set smile on her uncooperative mouth. 'I'm just a bit edgy.'

'I can't leave you like this,' he said harshly, urging her inside the door.

A scream of rosellas made her jump. Another garish flash of lightning lit up the room, outlining Keir as he strode across to pull the curtains.

'I'm not afraid,' she said, her voice muffled in the quiet room. 'Thunderstorms make me tense, but they don't really scare me.'

He was scaring her.

'Why?' he asked.

As more thunder mumbled around the sky she said, 'I don't know. They just do.'

'Perhaps because they remind you of the day in the bush when a storm came up and you and your friend ran screaming down the track beneath the kauri trees—the day you learned your mother would do anything to appease your stepfather. That's a hard lesson for a child to learn.'

Why had she told him that? Eyes almost black in her white face, she pressed her lips together and headed across to the sink. With shaking hands she turned on the tap and filled a glass with water. It slid down her dry throat as another flash of lightning ripped the cloud apart. Thunder blasted the taut silence, roaring down from the sky and up from the earth, elemental, ferocious, mindless.

Just the way she felt about Keir. Love no longer entered into it, if love ever had, but she was determined to exorcise that raw, basic need until she could look at Keir with nothing more than mild admiration for a sexy man.

Turning to face him, she gave him another tight smile. 'Be careful driving. We haven't had rain for well over a month so the roads will be slippery.'

Keir came across and lifted her chin, subjecting her to a cool, analytical stare. Heat crept into her skin, and her lashes fell.

'All right. I'll see you later,' he said, and let her go.

Hope waited until the door closed behind him before she drew breath.

As the lightning crackled and spat and the thunder rumbled overhead, she showered and changed into a knitted silk singlet top, a close match to the colour of her skin. With it she teamed black trousers and a pair of gold sandals, then made up carefully, emphasising her eyes with soft, golden-taupe shadow, filling in her lips with a honey-pink lipstick. She finished by spraying herself lightly with Les Belles de Ricci, hoping Keir liked the delicious citrus fragrance.

Perhaps she should have chosen something more discreet—no, she thought, frowning. If he didn't like her perfume he could say so and she might not wear it when she was with him, but second-guessing was a fast, degrading road to defeat. Her mother had turned it into a way of life.

She looked for a long moment at her reflection, noting the

glinting, gleaming eyes, the flush along her cheekbones, the soft curve of her mouth.

'I hope you know what you're doing,' she said to the golden woman in the mirror.

By the time Keir's car turned into the driveway again the thunder had grumbled its way north, taking with it the tumultuous shower that accompanied it. Newly washed palm fronds waved against a sky of tender blue, each green tress outlined by rain jewels, and birds were calling above the sound of running gutters.

Her stomach churning with anticipation, Hope ran down the steps and along the drive. Suddenly buoyant and alive, her skin flushed and sensitive, her spirits soaring, she drew in great lungfuls of fresh, clean, cool air.

Clad entirely in black, as lithely dangerous as a warrior, Keir got out and swung around to open the passenger door. His rapid, unsmiling survey set her tingling. 'My mother used to grow a rose with ferocious thorns, but the flowers glowed in the sun like living light and radiance. So do you.'

Stunned, Hope gazed at him with slightly parted lips. He gave her a mocking smile and his gaze dropped to her mouth. 'And if you keep looking at me like that,' he murmured, 'I'll carry you back inside...'

His voice, deep and mesmeric, dissolved every sinew and bone in her body, as did the widening darkness in his eyes, rimmed by ice and fire. Hypnotised, she tried to think of something to say—anything that would smash the tension and give her back her mind.

'But if I do that,' he said, with a quick, twisted smile, 'Philibert may never let us into his restaurant again, and that would be a pity.'

'Yes,' she muttered, recovering enough composure to scuttle into the car and barricade herself behind the seat belt while she watched him stride around the front of the car.

His shirt and trousers were cut with a spare elegance that

gave admiring homage to broad shoulders and narrow hips and long, muscular legs; he looked like some rakish, menacing fantasy of high romance, at once threatening and overwhelmingly sensual.

Hell, Hope thought feverishly, get a grip!

It took all of her energy to summon a calm voice, a light tone. Once he'd switched on the engine she asked, 'Are you on holiday, or working?'

'Working,' he said, smoothly putting the car in gear. He turned, slung an arm along the back of her seat, and began backing the vehicle down the drive.

Acutely, painfully aware of that strong arm only centimetres from her shoulders, she had to reorganise her churning thoughts. 'Someone said you're talking to a Chinese delegation.'

'Yes.'

'I hope it's going well.'

'So far, so good,' he said non-committally.

It was stupid to feel rebuffed; why should he tell her? Pushing down a tendril of hurt, she said brightly, 'Isn't it a glorious evening?'

'Fantastic,' he said, and sent her an oblique glance as he turned the wheel and the car joined the traffic at the end of the road. 'Breathtaking.'

Three hours later Hope gazed at an elaborate concoction of chocolate and strawberries with awe and real regret. 'No,' she sighed at the bald, mustachioed man who offered it, 'I would dearly love to, but I just haven't got the room for it.'

Philibert echoed her sigh. 'I made it especially for you,' he said sadly. 'When my good friend Keir rang to say that he was bringing a golden woman with a voice as lazy and lovely as the sound of a summer afternoon, not only did I cancel my other bookings, but I knew that I would make you this.' His dark eyes rested mournfully on her face.

Keir said dryly, 'Don't let that fake accent or the flowery language fool you—when we were at school together he played lock in the first fifteen.'

Philibert sighed again, even more fulsomely. 'Ah, those wonderful years of our youth.' He winked at Hope. 'Keir played fullback—and had all the girls drooling like drainpipes over him. I hated him. It's a wonder I let him come to my restaurant.'

The two men grinned at each other. Clearly great friends, they couldn't have been more different. Years of sampling his own exquisite cooking had made the chef rotund, and his genetic heritage had bestowed baldness on him. Beside him Keir looked younger, and infinitely, spectacularly, more magnetic.

'Are you sure you couldn't eat any of this—not even a delicious morsel?' Philibert wheedled. 'I am not allowed to eat it, and my darling wife doesn't touch puddings. It will be thrown away.'

'It's a wicked waste, but no,' Hope said regretfully. 'And I hope you didn't really cancel your other bookings.'

'For my friend—my *important* friend—of course!' He grinned at Keir, unawed by his wealth or power. 'The customers will come back because they know I am very, very exclusive, and part of the mystique is that booking is not enough. If a king comes for a private holiday to Noosa, then I tell my customers, sorry, no, tonight I have to cancel. Try again next month.'

'Hmm,' Hope said. 'So it's all a con?' She laughed at his outraged expression. 'Not the food, of course—that's sublime.'

Keir drawled, 'The problem is *becoming* exclusive; once you've got there you can do almost anything and the punters will still flock in. Mob psychology works every time. Make it difficult for people, and you'll have them hammering on your door.'

'Being the best cook in the southern hemisphere helps,' Philibert agreed without any false modesty, 'but it would have taken us much longer without my friend Keir. It helps to have a backer who's devious and cynical and knows how to manipulate our masters, the public. Now, if you're not going to eat this pudding, what are we going to do with it?'

Keir looked at Hope and said, 'Do you think Jaedan and Abby would like it?'

'Your children?' The chef's eyes darted to Hope, then switched to Keir's. With a spark of amused malice, he added, 'Keir's really good with kids.'

Hope told him, 'They're the kids next door.'

Philibert raised his eyebrows, but said, 'You must take it for them. Get them early, I always say.'

'Thank you.' She smiled at him. 'That was the most wonderful meal I've ever had in my life.'

'Of course,' he said with splendid insouciance.

Philibert's restaurant crouched on the edge of an inky dune lake, still and smooth, surrounded by the low, pale-trunked trees the Australians call wallum scrub. An immense darkness pressed against them; listening to the silence, Hope felt she understood a little of the mystery and age of this enormous, ancient continent.

The evening had been an experience she'd never forget. Yet although the food and wine had been magnificent, Keir had overshadowed their impact; enthralled by his potent, masculine charm, she'd been trapped in a dazzling spell.

'Coffee?' Philibert asked.

'Another storm's on the way,' Keir said, getting to his feet. 'They make Hope a bit nervous, so we'll head back to Noosa now.'

Philibert didn't try to press them. 'Then enjoy the rest of the evening.' He smiled at her. 'And stay in contact now that we know you.'

As they drove away, Hope eyed the stakes that indicated

the depth of any floodwater over the road. A slow, potent excitement built within her, making it difficult for her to control her tone. 'What made Philibert decide to live here?'

'He lives to cook, but he hates the organisation of a large kitchen. After he'd spent time in France and Singapore he came here for a holiday, and fell in love with the place and a local girl.'

'I gather you're his backer?'

'Yes. He deserved his chance. He and his wife have worked their hearts out getting to their present position '

'He's a superb cook, and that was a magical evening; thank you very much.' A slash of lightning at the edge of her vision made Hope stiffen. The white, fierce light vanished, to be followed by a roll of thunder and a sudden spatter of drops on the windscreen. 'More rain!'

'The locals keep apologising about the unusual weather.'

Long needles of rain lanced down, rapidly wetting the road. Hope usually worried about driving in these intense downpours, but she settled back into her seat, safe because Keir would know how to deal with it.

Unbidden, unwanted, a thought sneaked into her brain. Was this the way her mother had felt when she'd first met her father? He too was competent, a man you could trust in an emergency.

Not that it mattered, because she didn't plan to fall in love with Keir. Every time he looked at her she felt the impact of those ice-coloured eyes right through to her soul, but next week he'd be back in New Zealand, or wherever his headquarters were, and she'd be working out her notice, ready to move on again.

Shivering, she glanced at Keir's hands on the wheel. Lean, experienced. She could imagine them only too vividly against her skin.

'Cold?' he asked without taking his eyes off the road. 'Put on the heater if you want to.'

'I'm fine.'

They were almost in Noosa when he asked casually, 'Would you like a nightcap?'

'No, thank you.' Her voice sounded odd—both rough and languid. She cleared her throat and went on, 'I've eaten enough delicious food and drunk enough superb wine to last for months.'

As the car drew up outside the house she looked with some dismay at the rain. When Keir switched off the engine he said, 'Wait there. I have an umbrella.'

The engine died; in the glow of the headlights she saw him reach over into the back and produce a long black affair. 'Courtesy of the concierge,' he told her with a caged smile, and got out.

In the glow of the headlights he strode around and opened her door; pudding in hand, she scrambled out, and as the headlights clicked off he pulled her against him. Sheltered by the umbrella and his body from the rain, she tried to match his strides before realising that he was adjusting his to hers.

For once the top of the house was dark; her landlady's lights would have been a help.

She unlocked the door, switched on the light and hurried straight into the kitchen, depositing the pudding in the fridge. When she stood up again Keir had pushed the door closed and was coming across the room, focused on her with disturbing intensity.

Some time during the kiss Hope's heart flipped over and she lost whatever intelligence she'd been born with, yielding to the carnal hunger that smashed through her defences with the violence of the storm raging outside.

CHAPTER SEVEN

As HOPE's hands tightened onto his shoulders she gasped, 'Your shirt's wet...'

'To hell with my shirt,' Keir growled over the rumble of the rain, and found her mouth again.

This time she surrendered, opening to him, forgetting everything but the insistent drumming of need inside her, the vehement craving to take and give.

When his head lifted again she could no longer think. Yet he said harshly, 'Is this what you want, Hope? All of me, everything? Because if it isn't, we'd better stop now.'

Stop? How could he even think of banking this honeyed flame of desire? Not again, she thought fiercely, all doubts finally banished in an agony of need.

Lifting her hand, she traced the sculptured outline of his mouth. Beneath her fingertip she felt it shape a kiss; her shiver exploded into inner conflagration when he took the tip of her finger into his mouth and bit it gently.

Sensation scorched through her, kindling a needfire so violent it burned away the last rational promptings of her brain. If only she'd had some experience—but even that thought died, for she was glad she'd never felt like this before, never wanted like this.

Only Keir, and Keir was all her world...

'You're wet,' she said, her voice husky. 'Take off your shirt and I'll put it in the drier.'

'You take it off,' he said, narrowed eyes gleaming in his set face. He stepped back and held out his arms, challenging her in the most stark, basic way of all—the primitive sexual challenge of man to woman.

Take what you want, his tone, his expression said.

If you dare...

For a frozen second they stared at each other, eyes fencing across the space between them.

Then, clamping down on her leaping excitement, Hope lifted a deliberate hand. To the heavy thud of her heartbeats she leaned forward and began to undo the small buttons. Her fingers tingled, yearned for the sleek skin beneath, but she took her time, letting the dampness and texture and elusive male scent build her arousal. The quick rise and fall of his chest told her that her touch was having an equally potent effect on Keir.

'There,' she said quietly when she'd freed the last button.

'Thank you.' The words rasped, and he shrugged out of the garment, his wide shoulders gleaming with overt power in the subdued light.

Dry-mouthed with tension, Hope took the shirt into the minuscule bathroom and put it in the drier. She'd straightened up when another jagged slash of lightning ripped the sky apart, followed almost immediately by a crack of thunder that vibrated all around and through her.

Keir crossed the room in two silent strides, pulling her into the dangerous haven of his arms. The heat of his body enfolded her in a cocoon of primal reassurance as he said into her hair, 'There's nothing to be afraid of, Hope. You'll be safe.'

He wasn't speaking about the storm. His tantalising maleness—forceful strength, fine-grained, hair-textured skin—bypassed her conscious brain, activating a hidden female knowledge handed down through the generations.

Into the bulge of shoulder muscle she said, 'I'm not scared,' shivering as his skin tightened under each tiny kiss. That flash of fear had sharpened her senses to a feral acuteness; intense excitement bloomed as swiftly as a moonflower, unfolding its petals through her until she couldn't free herself of its wild vitality.

Bending, Keir kissed her throat. Against her clamouring skin his mouth was gentle yet demanding, as though he was afraid to unleash the power smouldering beneath his iron control.

'I'm not eighteen now,' she muttered.

His chest lifted sharply. 'Show me,' he challenged, eyes gleaming.

At first tentatively, then with more confidence, she explored the arrogant line of his profile with her fingertips, found the furry thickness of his lashes and the curved sweep of his cheekbones, shivered at the tactile sensuousness of the skin over his jaw and square chin, and the curled, elegant shape of his ear with its astoundingly soft lobe.

'Yes,' he said, his voice raw. His mouth moved from her throat to the juncture of her neck and her shoulder; there, with infinitely erotic restraint, his strong white teeth closed onto the skin.

Hope flinched. Such a tiny caress to conjure primitive wantonness in her!

Harshly, Keir demanded, 'Did I hurt you?'

'No.' Copying him, she bit into the coiled swell of his shoulder, and then licked it, relishing the tang of salt and the scent—purely masculine with a fresh hint of rain.

His mouth found hers again with an unslaked, ferocious insistence. Yielding her first barricade, Hope opened her lips to his passionate mastery. Her hands clenched onto hot skin, stretched taut over tense muscles, and she pressed against him, eager for the power of his body, joyous when she felt the involuntary thrust of his loins.

A low, harsh sound grated in his throat; he pulled her singlet top above her shoulders and lowered his mouth to the skin he had bared.

The light silk across her face emphasised each sensation.

Skilful, knowledgeable, his kisses summoned fire. Blind and deaf to everything but the astonishing rapture of his lips against her breast, Hope groaned.

With slow, sensual torment, he found his way to the aching, eager centre. Hope's head fell back in an agony of anticipation as his mouth unleashed an untamed, incandescent excitement; tossed by the delirium of pleasure, she felt herself melting, loosening, and yet the need to stretch and tighten almost overwhelmed her.

'You are so beautiful,' he growled. 'Honey and fire and spice, sweet as flowers and strong as diamonds...'

Straightening, he flicked the singlet over her head and picked her up and buried his face in her breasts, holding her with barely curbed strength as though fighting for control.

The light snapped off, imprisoning them in a cell of deafening darkness. Jolted into an old childhood nightmare, Hope felt her body clench, but Keir was there with her, his ardent hands supporting her, his presence a cloak against the darkness.

The only sounds she could hear were the pounding of his heart and the harsh intake of his breath. Against her newly aware skin she felt the soft abrasion of his jaw.

'Keir,' she said aloud, her voice thick and slow, creamy with desire.

Curving her fingers, she ran her nails lightly from his throat through the fine hair across his chest, down the iron-muscled torso—marking him, staking her claim in the most fundamental way she knew.

'No.' The word was flat and constricted. He caught her hand and yanked it away from his flat belly. 'Let me do this my way. Afterwards you can do what you like to me, but if you touch me this will be short and brutal, and I want to take you long and slow until you die of pleasure, until you can no longer speak or think or do anything but feel.'

Huskily, barely able to articulate, she murmured, 'Whatever you do—short and brutal or long and slow—you won't hurt me.'

His arms bunched around her but the pressure didn't increase. 'Don't argue.'

He wasn't going to give in. Smiling, she lifted her head and kissed him, shaping her mouth to his.

Keir laughed, the short, triumphant laugh of a lover, and held her against him while he yanked back the bedcover and said, 'Lie down for me, you beautiful creature.'

But she perched on the edge of the bed, glad of the kindly darkness yet wishing she could glory in him as he stripped.

Should she do the same? Embarrassment warred with modesty; in the end she stayed in her silky trousers, her hands linked tightly in her lap. Against the resumed growl of thunder, rapid-fire flashes of lightning revealed tantalising glimpses of long legs and narrow masculine hips, of bronzed shoulders that could shut out the world, and the fascinating scroll of hair across his chest.

Savouring each brief glimpse, storing it in her mind against a lonely future, Hope thought, I'll never be nervous of lightning again.

Besides the heady anticipation she recognised another emotion—uncertainty about the unknown. So impressive was Keir's size and his powerful, lithe strength and grace that she wondered whether she was going to be able to satisfy him.

He thought he was making love to an experienced woman. He was going to get a virgin.

Perhaps her stillness warned him, for when he was naked he sat down beside her, not very close, and ran his hand from her mouth to her waist in a caress deliberately modelled on hers. Only he didn't use his nails; he stroked with the pads of his fingers so lightly that it was like the lightest brush of a feather.

Unbearably aroused, Hope shivered beneath that tender,

knowledgeable caress, but she didn't—couldn't—move, couldn't respond.

Audaciously Keir traced with his mouth the route of his fingers, pushing her gently backwards and easing down her trousers. Eventually his lips reached the small cup of her navel.

Slow shudders ran the length of her spine, gathered and intensified in the pit of her stomach. Wide-eyed, she twisted under his measured, lazy exploration. Nobody had told her that her navel was connected by white-hot nerves to that secret passage between her thighs, or that a kiss there could soften her bones and cloud her mind.

'You taste like flowers and wine,' he said against the gentle curve of her stomach, and deftly peeled back her trousers, taking her briefs with them so that she lay before him as naked as he was, her body storming into exultation.

The thunder was moving away, the lightning less garish in the darkened room. Hope's shallow, rapid breathing resounded in her ears. She put out a shy hand and touched his hip, smoothing over the jut of bone and down the muscular thigh.

'Not yet,' he said, a jagged undercurrent roughening his voice.

But she wasn't content to lie like a doll. For answer she ran a fingertip from his hip to his nipple, and from there to his solar plexus, the centre of his chest. His heart raced beneath her questing palm; she liked that, enjoyed her power to move him.

Abruptly he bent and kissed her, deeply, deliberately, with such sexual confidence that for a fleeting moment Hope wished he was as unpractised at this as she was.

Afterwards she could never remember the exact sequence of events; Keir wove about her a sensuous thrall that kept her constantly afire with new sensations. Dazzled and bewildered by her unleashed responses, she discovered the many and various pleasure points in her body.

Not only a skilful and considerate lover, he made the outrageous seem inevitable and infinitely seductive, until at last he moved over her and eased himself gently into the panting, shaking body he'd prepared with his accomplished mouth and his knowledgeable hands.

Hope had heard that it often hurt the first time, but she was lucky; although acutely stretched, she was so lost in carnal delight that she accommodated him, and found that sometimes there was no end to pleasure.

'No,' he said in a heavy, labouring voice. 'Stay still.'

She froze.

On a ghost of a laugh, a humourless catch of breath, he said, 'You're going to kill me with—' He stopped, then resumed, 'I'm not going to last if you move, and I want to make it...'

When his voice tailed off she looked up with night-attuned eyes.

Beads of sweat stood out on his brow as he said through gritted teeth, 'I want to make it perfect for you,' and pushed deep, deep inside her, taking her with one flowing thrust delivered with all his force.

A voice cried out; astonished, Hope realised it was hers. Although she tried to stay still she couldn't prevent the instinctive, mindless rhythm of her hips as her body arched to meet him and enclose him, take him into her. Linking arms and legs around him, she met his thrusts with her own in a powerful, age-old union that both gave and took, joined and separated, growing more and more heated until she was aware only of sensation, pure and intense and violently rapturous in every cell of her body.

Yet she sensed that there was still something missing, even though she didn't know what it was. Beyond this ferocious pleasure lay another height, another pleasure even more intense. Her mind didn't fully understand, but her body obeyed an imperative older than thought, older than consciousness; she tensed as Keir thrust again and again, hard and fast and deeply.

Slow waves gathered between them, spread through her, then suddenly exploded, filling her with an anguished ecstasy that only increased when he cried out and poured himself into her.

And then it was over—too brief, too sudden rapture—and she came down to the sound of rain and the feel of him as he turned on his side and held her against his chest so that she rose and fell with it as he fought for breath.

Stupid tears ached behind her eyes. From now on she'd never be able to enjoy the rain at night without remembering this transcendental experience.

'It's called post-coital blues,' he said, startling her as he kissed her damp lashes.

'I don't like it,' she retorted childishly, unable to think of anything intelligent to say. 'I thought you were supposed to be sleepy and sated after sex.'

And a tiny voice in her mind mocked, Oh, clever Hope—you've just admitted that you've never done this before!

'Some people are. Some cry. Why didn't you tell me you were a virgin?'

Had he realised before she'd betrayed herself? She peered at him, able to make out every harsh contour of his face—everything but the expression in his ice-grey eyes. 'Does it matter?'

There was no pat answer. He thought about it before saying, 'If I'd known I wouldn't have been so brutal.'

'You weren't brutal,' she protested, appalled. 'It was wonderful. What was it like for you?'

He laughed quietly and kissed the corner of her mouth. 'Transcendental. But you have nothing to compare it with.'

Hope's confidence surged back. 'Perhaps I should gain

some experience,' she suggested demurely, 'so I *can* make comparisons.'

There was a moment's silence before he drawled, 'Perhaps you should. Let's see what we can do, shall we?'

She'd thought nothing could top the sensations of their first lovemaking, but during that long night Keir showed her that there were infinite variations, infinite degrees of pleasure, infinite graduations of sexuality.

And when at last he left her, she lay rigid and desperate, clamping her eyes shut so that she couldn't see the grey light of dawn.

Defiantly, deliberately, she'd opened the Pandora's box of sexual awareness, but for her no hope lurked in the bottom. Keir was going to leave, and although she wouldn't have it any other way, she'd miss him with every cell in her body.

The rain had long gone by the time the sun came up on a bleak day by Noosa standards, with a cool westerly polishing the sky to pallor; palms rustled and crackled under the wind's sway as Hope walked to work. The cafés, usually full of people determined to squeeze every drop of pleasure from their holiday, were half empty.

She loved the little town, had fallen under its special spell of bush and sea and the exquisite beach, its brash, cheerful holiday ambience, and yet she thought, When I go I'll never come here again.

Late in the morning Chloe muttered, 'He's back. And looking for you.'

Heart thumping in a complicated rhythm, Hope looked up. Yes, it was Keir, dressed in clothes that managed to be both casual and formal, his expression withdrawn, the pale eyes hooded. Grave-faced, she went to meet him.

'I need to see you,' he said quietly.

She glanced at her watch. 'In half an hour?'

Unusually for him, he paused before saying, 'All right.'

Half an hour later, outside the shop, he said, 'Come up to my apartment.'

It was Hope's turn to hesitate, but she could tell from his aloofness that he wasn't planning a lovers' tryst. Hollow and empty of emotion, she nodded and walked along the street with him.

His suite was like Noosa, chic and subtropical and sophisticated. Hope walked across to the window. Beyond Double Island to the north lay mysterious Fraser Island, and the long, lazy coastline of south Queensland, stretching in voluptuous gold, green and blue towards the tropics. On the vivid grass below a black and white bird paced across the lawn, twitching its tail feathers from side to side like a woman managing a train-encumbered evening gown.

Fixing her eyes on the flicking feathers, she said, 'Fantastic view.' Her voice sounded flat, mechanical.

'I'm not talking to your back,' Keir said, a steely thread of aggression in his voice.

Hope sat down in one of the elegant wicker chairs, crossed her ankles and folded her hands in her lap. Fixing her gaze on his shirt pocket, she willed herself to stay still, stay quiet.

He said, 'I have to go to New York—there's a problem, and people are depending on me. I'm booked to fly out in half an hour.'

She nodded. Silence, oppressive and thick, blanketed the room. Unable to resist, she flicked a glance upwards.

'I'll be back.' Narrow, winter-coloured eyes searched hers.

Odd, she thought distantly, how easy it was to crack a heart. A one-night stand could do it. 'When?' Yes, that sounded all right—a bit remote, but normal.

He reached her before she could move, pulling her up from the chair with hands that wouldn't be denied.

'Running again, Hope?' Eyes gleaming, he surveyed her face. Softly, silkily, he continued, 'You beautiful, stubborn coward, you're no more immune to me than I am to you. I don't know how long it'll take me to sort out this mess in New York—no more than a week at the most—and I'll come back as soon as I can. And then we'll talk. Just remember this—last night you gave yourself to me and I'm not going to let you run away again.'

Dimly surprised that she could still function, that the words emerged without a tremor, she said, 'One night in my bed gives you no authority over me. I don't like macho, overbearing men who think they have the right to order women's lives for them.'

He frowned, half-closed eyes giving him an air of concentrated determination. Beneath the taut bronzed skin the autocratic framework intensified his emotion as he said evenly, 'Do you want me to plead with you to stay?'

'No!' She reached out and touched his face, cupping his cheek. Her skin tingled at rough silk beneath her palm and her fingertips—a sizzle of electricity that transformed her anger into helpless, compulsive desire. 'I'll be here when you come back,' she said quietly, making a decision she knew already was going to cost her pain.

Keir closed his eyes for a second. 'I'm sorry. Not just for being stupid, but for setting off old alarm bells.'

He meant her father, but she didn't have time to process this thought because he bent and kissed her, one hand snaking up to hold her head still. At first his mouth was gentle, and then the kiss transmuted, became hard, passionate, unsparing.

Arms looping his neck, Hope surrendered to the hunger he'd learned so well to arouse, giving him everything he asked for.

At last his head lifted and he surveyed her flushed face and amber eyes, dazed and heavy-lidded, the trembling, seeking mouth. A rough sound lifted his chest and he kissed her again with a hunted desperation that tore at her heart, only lifting his head at a discreet tap on the door.

'That will be Aline,' he said hoarsely, and let her go and strode across to the door.

Fiercely glad that he didn't ask his colleague inside, Hope dragged in a shuddering breath and concentrated on staying upright as Keir and Aline held a rapid, low-voiced conversation in the hall.

At the sound of the door being jerked shut she said in a brittle voice, 'I have to go; I said I'd be back as soon as I could.'

After a glance at his set, implacable expression, she summoned steel to her backbone and headed past him towards the door.

'Hope.'

She shook her head, but he reached for her again, and again she couldn't deny him. This kiss went on and on, fuelled by a deep, hungry need that intensified with each frustrating moment.

Eventually she wrenched her face sideways, breaking contact. 'I do have to go,' she whispered unsteadily.

'So do I.' But he didn't release her. Tucking her head under his chin, he went on, 'Wait for me to come back.'

There wasn't anything he could ask for that she wouldn't give.

'I promise.' Her voice sounded husky with longing, with conviction. Desperate, she pulled away.

This time he let her go and hauled a slim leather wallet from his pocket. Unfolding it, he flicked out a card, took a pen and scribbled something.

'Here's my home address and number,' he said. 'If you need me at all, ring. I might not be there, but whoever answers will know who you are and they'll know how to contact me.'

Without looking at it, Hope took the card. 'Don't come down with me.'

After a glance at her face he said, 'All right.' Another

knock on the door broke impatiently into the words he was going to say; his face darkening, he swore beneath his breath.

'Have a good trip,' Hope said, and pushed past a startled porter, escaping into the lift.

Keir came back after four days, arriving just as she was thinking of going to bed on Friday night. All day she'd been edgy, her nerves plucked by some baseless tension. When she heard the knock on the door she knew immediately that it was Keir; perhaps a spark of awareness, of wordless communication, had leapt across the distance between them to warn her he was on his way.

She opened the door and he asked, 'Don't you have a chain for this?'

'Yes.' Her body loosened, heated. She met eyes as clear and brilliant as diamond chips in a face carved into angles by a fiercely prowling sexuality. His hunger beat through the air, rousing her own so that her breasts tightened and her body tensed.

He slammed the door behind him, slid the chain across and said, 'Use it in future.'

'Yes, sir.'

The hard line of his mouth relaxed. 'Otherwise I'll worry,' he said deeply, and bent and kissed her.

Somehow they made it to the bed, but although he managed to use protection he still had his shirt on when he finally thrust deeply into her, and her jeans were dangling from her ankles.

The primitive intensity of their lovemaking, the stark, untamed power they created together, summoned such a wild response that Hope crested almost immediately, muffling her guttural cry in his shoulder. Uncontrollable rapture scorched through her, spinning her into a climax so intense, so perfect that she barely registered the moment when Keir flung his head back and reached his. Shattered by exquisite pleasure, by aching emptiness, she began to cry.

His big body coiled and flexed as he rolled over onto his side, taking her with him, manoeuvring her so that her head came to rest on his shoulder. His voice rumbled beneath her cheek. 'Are you going to do this after every time we make love?'

'I hope not,' she muttered, the words clogged with a bewildering mix of emotions. 'I don't know why. I—I never cry!'

He stroked the damp strands of her hair back from her face, his fingers sifting each lock, smoothing it back with such care and finesse that it felt like tenderness. 'Perhaps you'll be able to stop when you get used to making love.'

I hope so. But she didn't say the words aloud. That, after all, was the whole idea of the exercise—to get used to him. Ignoring the shiver scudding down her spine, she murmured on a yawn, 'Perhaps.'

'Mmm.' A finger traced the line of her lips, the shape of her nose, the thick lashes. He bent and kissed away the lingering moisture of her tears.

Hope sighed.

Amusement textured his deep voice. 'We'd better take a few clothes off before we go to sleep. I don't mind spending the night in my shirt, but you might find those jeans a bit of a nuisance.'

'I need a shower,' she muttered, suddenly afflicted with belated modesty.

'Me, too. I've been travelling for thirty hours.'

She blurted, 'You go first. You must be exhausted.'

After a moment he said, 'No, I'll wait.'

Shyly, she kicked off her jeans and walked naked across to the wardrobe. When she'd found her dressing gown she turned, and her breath blocked her throat. Keir had moved over onto his back, taking up the whole bed and filling the room with his powerful presence—a fascinating mixture of the energy inherent in every masculine curve and angle and line of his lean, graceful body.

Hope stopped, her eyes lingering on the symmetry of wide shoulders and strong arms, of sleek tanned skin and the classic pattern of hair across his chest. Slowly, her voice thick and hesitant, she said, 'I wish I was an artist. You're so beautiful.'

To her astonishment colour heated the high, stark cheekbones. 'In the eye of the beholder.'

'Modesty doesn't become you.'

Laughter glinted beneath his dark lashes, and she saw his shaft stir and thicken. 'If you want to shower you'd better go before I drag you back here.'

Scarlet-faced, she shot into the bathroom and showered quickly, taking a sweet, furtive pleasure in setting out a towel and toiletries for him. When she got back he'd straightened the sheets and had pulled his trousers on.

A muffled sound from above drew both their eyes to the ceiling.

'It's my landlady,' Hope said, colouring again. 'She's a light sleeper.'

He looked at her with hooded eyes. 'Pack a bag and come with me.'

She hesitated. He made no move to persuade her, but she could feel his determination reach out, enclosing her in the brutal force of his will-power. You want to get him out of your system, logic reminded her. Better if you're with him all the time.

Slowly she said, 'Yes, all right.'

He gave her a keen look, then nodded and went into the shower.

Her surrender chipped away at the independence she'd constructed so carefully over the years. It's in a good cause, she reminded herself as the shower sounded again and she hauled down a bag. For a greater freedom.

So why did she feel as though she was sliding further and further into danger? She'd be perfectly safe; once she'd rid herself of this physical obsession she'd see him for the man he really was—sensual, clever, a heart-shakingly magnificent lover, but a mere man just the same, not the mythical being she'd built in her mind, who possessed an erotic power over her that reeked of black magic.

A mere man who had betrayed her spectacularly, she reminded herself forcefully—a ruthless man who'd used her to get close to her father so he could take James Sanderson down—a hard man who fitted the word 'dominant' as though he'd been born to it. Mouth pulled into a straight, tense line, Hope set herself to decide just what clothes a woman should pack for a feverish sexual interlude.

She opened the drawer and frowned at her perfectly decent, perfectly sensible underwear. Pretty—but oh for something wildly sexy in silk!

The shower switched off. Still clad in her cotton dressing gown, Hope hissed with dismay and dragged on the first bra and briefs she came to before flying across to the wardrobe, hauling out a shirt and a pair of trousers and struggling into them. She piled underwear and a few of her more decent casual clothes higgledy-piggledy into the bag, and was brushing her hair when Keir came in, once more clad in trousers and shirt.

'I just need a few things from the bathroom,' she muttered, dropping the brush into her bag and easing past him to collect her toiletries.

'Are you working tomorrow?' he asked when she re-emerged.

'No. I've got the whole weekend off.'

Something kindled in his eyes. 'Then let's go.'

Instead of taking her to a hotel he drove along the road

towards the National Park, finally pulling into the driveway of a house that perched on the seaward side.

'It belongs to a friend,' he said as he hooked her bag from the back of the car. 'I thought you'd prefer it.'

He was right.

In an amused voice he said, 'Now, what did I say to cause that frown?'

'Nothing.' But Hope didn't want him understanding her. Their relationship had nothing to do with minds and emotions; it was about physical satiation. 'Nothing at all,' she said sturdily, and walked from the garage into the house beside him.

They spent the weekend in the house, most of it in bed. In those two days and three nights Hope, a shamelessly willing pupil, discovered that her body was capable of even more graduations of sexuality. Keir taught her the delights of earthiness; as well, she learned sophisticated techniques for increasing pleasure, and revelled in satisfying the swift, uncomplicated hunger that overtook them so often.

Once she had wondered how to seduce him; by the end of that weekend she knew his body so intimately she would never forget his sheer physicality, from the luxuriant way he stretched first thing in the morning to the blatant male power with which he overwhelmed her senses when they made love.

And that happened often. He turned everything into an occasion for lovemaking, seducing her in the kitchen when they cooked dinner, in the sitting room on the rug, and much later in the pool, when he brought her to an orgasm that terrified her with its intensity.

Not once did they read a newspaper or turn on the television set or leave the property, but he did introduce her to billiards, at which she discovered a surprising talent, and they played tennis and vicious games of poker and listened to a state-of-the-art music system.

He knew a lot more about music than she did. Hope realised that it was his greatest joy, one of the few things that helped him relax and forget his business empire.

Another was when they made love. Then he concentrated only on her response and her body. She learned how to pleasure him, that when she ran the tips of her fingernails down his spine he rolled over instantly ready for her; she committed his scent to memory, the smooth glide of his skin was imprinted deep in her cells, the deep, raspy texture of his morning voice would never leave her ears.

She discovered that he knew when to be considerate and gentle, and when to treat her with a forceful, unsparing hunger that never degenerated into roughness or cruelty.

She found out that she was insatiable for him, even when she was tired, even when he woke her in the middle of the night and made love to her in a swathe of moonlight. He had only to touch her, she had only to hear his voice, and she wanted him.

Her plan, she thought starkly on the last day, eyeing the small package she'd found under her pillow, to immunise herself against him had failed miserably.

'What is it?' she asked.

'Open it and see.'

Although it was still early in the morning he was dressed, as was she. They'd woken before dawn and made love with a tinge of desperation because he had to catch a plane.

Panic hollowing out her stomach, she finally managed to get the package open. It was a jeweller's box. When she cast him a furious look he laughed, and came over and sat down beside her on the bed.

'No,' he said, a lean hand holding her fingers closed on the box, 'it's not payment, and it's not some sort of trophy. I saw it and knew it was yours.' His voice deepened, a raw intensity roughening the words. 'I imagined making love to you with it on.'

Two days and three nights of excess, yet at that tone Hope's breath still caught in her throat. Slowly she opened the case. A single stone winked fire at her, golden and incandescent as the heart of the sun. A thin, exquisitely worked chain slid through her fingers; slowly she looped it over her head and let the stone fall into the hollow between her breasts.

'What is it?' she asked, feeling its cool weight against her heart.

'A miniature sun for a summer woman,' he said, and bent and kissed the spot the stone covered. 'A canary diamond. I knew what it would look like on you. Wear it and think of me when I'm gone. I'll be back in a month.'

That was when Hope knew she'd have to run.

CHAPTER EIGHT

THE next fortnight passed in a haze of bleak activity; both dreading and hoping that Keir would come back before she left, Hope organised her departure from Noosa.

'But *why* are you going?' Val demanded on the last day, slapping a mug of tea onto the table in front of her. 'You haven't given me a sensible reason yet. I thought you liked it here?'

'I do.'

Val got up to check on the children in the pool. Turning back, she said, 'It's Keir, I suppose. What went wrong? Don't tell me you're going to dump him like you have the others?'

'I didn't dump the others! They were just friends.'

Val snorted. 'Who wanted very much to be much more than friends, only you wouldn't have it. I could understand that because you certainly weren't in love—or even in lust— with them. But Keir was different. You glowed when you were with him.'

'It didn't mean anything,' Hope told her crisply, drinking down some of the tea while she tried to convince herself that she'd be once more in control of her life—and herself—as soon as she got away from this place.

The older woman gave her a baffled stare. However, something in Hope's expression must have warned her off, because she came across to the table and gave her a quick hug. 'All right, I won't pry. Just give me your address, all right? Otherwise I'll worry.'

'As soon as I settle in I'll write. I promise.'

Back in the flat, Hope looked around. Her belongings stood packed in one large pack and a box. Perhaps Val's

121

robust disapproval had found a weak spot, because she was listening to the honeyed voice of temptation again.

Why not wait for Keir to come back? Those days and nights of incredible rapture hadn't really been enough to liberate herself from his spell. If she stayed in Noosa he might visit her often enough for the novelty to fade, and then—when she could look at Keir Carmichael and see just another sexy, interesting man—then she'd be able to let her dreams go.

No! With shaking hands she picked up the three cards he'd sent her since he'd left Noosa. She'd planned to throw them in the rubbish, but she couldn't.

If she saw any more of him she might as well hand her heart on a plate to a man she didn't dare trust.

Yet she wanted—longed!—to have faith in his integrity. The inevitable next step, she thought bleakly, would be love, the abject surrender that had ruined her mother's life.

She'd been so conceited, so arrogant to believe she could keep herself safe while she indulged in rapturous sex with Keir.

Her fingers curled protectively around the cards as she stowed them in her bag. Monumentally stupid she might have been, but even she could learn her lesson. She'd never allow herself to be dominated by a man, not even a man who made her body sing with ecstasy and challenged her mind in a thousand absorbing ways.

He would call it cowardice; she called it self-preservation.

So she said goodbye to the Petries and her landlady, and travelled drearily by bus to the Gold Coast, another holiday destination an hour south of Brisbane, one big enough to hide her for as long as it took Keir to lose interest.

Once there she operated on automatic pilot, renting a small flat well back from the superb beach that gave the city of Surfers' Paradise its name. Within a week she was employed by a house-cleaning service. It was hard work but reasonably well paid, and because most of the home-owners were out during the day she had plenty of lonely hours to miss Keir while she vacuumed and mopped and cleaned and scanned the Situations Vacant columns for a better job.

It didn't help to tell herself that she'd get over this astonishing pain, that time healed all things. Time certainly hadn't healed her when she'd run away from him before—she'd survived only by repressing the memories.

This time she had to tough it out.

But she spent the nights lying awake, listening to her thoughts scurrying around her head, weighed down by the ache in her heart. During the day, she had to push her heavy limbs to work, to walk to the supermarket, to clean her own flat. Because food tasted like ashes, she ate only enough to keep going.

One morning her neighbour, a middle-aged woman, turned the key in her lock at the same time that Hope was setting out for another day's work.

'Are you all right?' the older woman asked, scrutinising Hope's face. 'You're very pale.'

'Just a bit tired,' Hope said quickly, smiling to show she wasn't offended.

'You could have the flu,' her neighbour observed, frowning. 'There's a nasty virus going around—no real symptoms except for exhaustion.'

'I've been thinking of buying some vitamins.' Hope picked up her bag and stepped down onto the common driveway.

'Take my advice and go to a doctor. It can't do any harm, and at least then you'll find out what you've got. There's a good medical centre in the shopping centre just along the road.'

Hope had no intention of visiting a medical centre—until she fainted getting out of bed next morning. She came to immediately, but it worried her enough to make an appointment and keep it on her way home from work.

A young woman doctor examined her, took her blood pressure, peered in her throat and ears, and listened to her chest and back. Afterwards she sat down behind her desk and asked bluntly, 'Could you be pregnant?'

'No,' Hope said explosively, her stomach quivering. 'I—we—took precautions.'

'If the precautions you took were just condoms, there's a definite possibility,' the doctor informed her dryly, and sent her off to the practice nurse for a pregnancy test.

Twenty minutes later the doctor told her, not unsympathetically, 'You're pregnant. When was the date of your last period?'

Numbly Hope counted back the weeks and told her.

The doctor nodded and looked down at a paper on her desk. 'The baby's due the first week in May.'

'I see.' Hope swallowed.

'Unless, of course, you choose to—'

'No.' Hope didn't even have to think about it. 'No, thank you. Is there anything special I should do or shouldn't do?'

The doctor took her medical history, told her what she should do, prescribed vitamins and as much rest as she could take, and gave her a diet sheet.

On the way back to the flat Hope detoured into a park shaded by African tulip trees and subtropical shrubs; small, white-beaked coots swam in a pond and black-headed ibises stalked the margins, looking vaguely sinister.

Hope sat down on a seat and touched her stomach with a wondering hand. Somewhere in there—so tiny it barely existed—was her child, the child she'd conceived when Keir and she had made love. A stab of exultant joy persuaded her to picture his baby in her arms, to wonder if it would have his pale eyes and black hair, that elegant, careless grace...

Not that it mattered whether their son or daughter looked like him or inherited her features and tawny colouring. Alight with fierce, inconvenient love for the tiny life within, she whispered, 'Don't worry, little one—you're safe, I promise.'

And then she wrenched herself reluctantly away from the tender daydream and forced herself to be pragmatic, clenching her hands together in her lap as she tried to work out what would be best for the precious child she carried.

Once it was born she'd be imprisoned by its dependence and her love. There'd be no escape; she might achieve some sort of freedom after the child had grown up, but for the rest of her life she'd be the mother to Keir's child.

Panic threatened to block her thought processes, but she forced herself past that first, unreasoning reaction. Her own wishes, her own needs, were no longer paramount.

Should she tell Keir?

No. He'd want to have some part in its life.

He'd take over.

And the way she felt now, she thought wearily, she'd probably let him. Of course, she might wake up the following morning feeling as fit as she ever had; apparently that was as likely to happen as the three months of exhaustion she'd been warned about.

She wouldn't tell Keir. Not because she didn't trust him, but because she didn't trust herself; the temptation to give in to his authority and decisiveness wooed her seductively. She needed time to come to terms with this.

'Hope, I'm sorry, but it's not working out.' The owner of the cleaning service was matter-of-fact. 'I can't afford to employ anyone who's not pulling their weight, and you haven't been.'

Hope stiffened her backbone. 'I know,' she said numbly. Strange that she should feel so shattered, because she'd been expecting this.

'Are you all right?'

'Yes.' She gave the woman a small smile. 'I'm pregnant.'

'Oh, Lord, I remember that tiredness.' The woman looked sympathetic, but she wasn't going to change her mind. 'Right, I'll give you a fortnight's wages in lieu of notice. Good luck with the baby—and everything.'

Once I get to the flat, Hope told herself as she signed for the wages and got herself out of the office, I can fall to pieces—for ten minutes or so, until I work out what to do.

A fierce, overwhelming protectiveness stiffened her body, propelled her home. She'd coped with everything life had flung at her so far; she'd cope with this.

But back in her stuffy little sitting room she sat in the only comfortable armchair and let herself drift into welcoming oblivion.

She woke so thirsty her throat felt like a desert, and so tired it was an enormous effort to get up and pour herself a glass of water.

Standing in front of the elderly refrigerator, she accepted the decision her mind had somehow arrived at in her sleep. With only the equivalent of three months' salary in the bank, plus pending payment for two travel articles, finding cheaper accommodation was her next step. Her best bet would be in a low-income suburb of Brisbane; failing that, a small town in Australia's vast, dusty hinterland.

Unexpected homesickness blitzed her. Here the sun beamed down through perfumed air, the life was casual and friendly. In New Zealand spring would be chilly, windy, frequently wet, yet the grass was a green she'd never seen in Australia. Pansies and violas and linarias—her mother's favourite annuals—would be brightening the gardens now. The winds would be blowing the strong, evocative scent of freesias along the streets, and there'd be daffodils, and Japanese cherries in their brief, delicate finery, and fruit trees awash in pink and white blossom.

It was the season for tangelos, sweet and gaudily orange on glossy bushes, and tamarillos, like oval tomatoes in clusters on their big-leafed trees—tangy and ruby-red. And, spread around its twin harbours, Auckland would shine on the fine spring days like a city seen in paradise.

But if she went back to New Zealand she'd be much easier for Keir to find.

Always provided he was looking for her, of course.

Perhaps she shouldn't have sent the diamond pendant back to him. If she'd kept it she could have sold it through Markus, and then she'd have had enough to live on for some years.

Shaking her head impatiently, she gulped the cold water down, then ran her wrists under the tap. She'd never take anything for herself from Keir. But the baby was different. Watching the water splash and foam over her blue veins, she accepted with enormous reluctance that she'd have to contact him.

Independence was all very well, but she didn't just have herself to think of now.

Now you understand the power of sex, she thought, trying desperately for irony, almost gagging at the bitterness of the lie. Because it hadn't been just sex.

Making love to Keir had forged bonds of passion and need and longing—bonds that now locked her inside a cage of her own making.

At least she'd had the sense to get out before she'd fallen in love with him, she thought fiercely.

An abrupt knock jerked her head around. Through the frosted glass panel of the door she saw the threatening silhouette of a tall man. A whirling darkness threatened, was beaten back as she wondered half hysterically if she'd summoned him with her thoughts.

Ashen-faced, determined, she used every atom of willpower she possessed to square her shoulders and walk across the room. Her fingers shook on the door handle; swallowing, she gripped it and pulled the door open.

The sight of Keir—alarmingly large and all coiled, furious

aggression, silver eyes unreadable in a hard-edged face—jolted apprehension through her, chilling her skin and roiling her stomach.

'Come in,' she said with the best imitation she could produce of her usual crisp tone.

Noiselessly he strode through the door and closed it behind him, his eyes never leaving her. 'What's the matter with you?'

'Nothing.' She must, she thought thinly, look like something pale and sluggish from off a cave wall. And although she was both angry and despairing, a huge weight had rolled off her shoulders.

'You look bloody awful,' he said grimly. 'Have you been sick?'

'No.' Tell him, she urged herself, but she couldn't think of any way to do it.

Silence hung as menacing as a thundercloud, broken by his savage question. 'Why the hell did you leave Noosa? And why didn't you contact Val Petrie—she was frantic with worry until she got your note.'

'Have you been hounding her?' Hope's lassitude vanished as though he'd brought the elixir of life with him. 'How dare you? Who do you think you are?'

'I'm your lover,' he said brutally, 'the lover you ran from. Why, Hope? Did your appalling stepfather make you so terrified of any sort of commitment that you had to run away?'

'What commitment?' she fired back. She caught up the bitter words on a deep breath. Forcing her voice to steady, she resumed, 'I found out that I'm a lousy mistress. I'm too used to my independence to wait around for a man. Why not just agree that we had a good time together and leave it at that?'

'Can you?' he asked lethally. 'You only had to say if you wanted to make something more of our relationship.'

'I didn't!'

'Make up your mind,' he said with cruel mockery. 'If it was money you wanted—'

Goaded into stupidity, she swung at him, regretting it instantly as one swift lean hand broke the blow, fastened around her wrist and hauled her into the heat and power of his poised warrior's body.

Eyes glittering, mouth fiercely disciplined into a hard, straight line, he said, 'I always knew you'd have a temper.'

'Of course I have a temper.' Her brain was drifting, spinning, and she couldn't drag her eyes away from the piercing intensity of his. 'Keir,' she breathed, her muscles loosening, her body preparing itself for his triumphant penetration. She licked dry lips, and saw with a fierce pang of pleasure the way his pupils narrowed, the gleaming shards of crystal heated by a reciprocal surge of desire, the heaviness of his eyelids as they lowered.

Then he let her go and stood back.

Chilled, she swayed, and grabbed the back of the nearest chair.

'So,' he said silkily, 'what do we do now, Hope?'

Before she could change her mind, she rapped out, 'I'm pregnant. I've just found out.'

Mutely she watched every bit of expression leach out of his face, watched the light die in his eyes; her eyes noted the sudden flick of a muscle in his jaw. He didn't move, and she couldn't breathe.

When he spoke she almost collapsed with the release of tension.

'I see,' he said remotely. 'When is it due?'

She told him and he nodded, those cold, implacable eyes surveying her as though he could somehow see the baby—his baby. 'You've lost weight. Are you suffering from morning sickness?'

'Not exactly.'

'Then *what*, exactly?' he demanded.

'I don't feel like eating, but I'm not sick. And I'm exhausted all the time, but apparently that's quite normal. I'm not sleeping very well—that's probably the heat, although I should be used to it by now.' Firmly, before she could babble any more, she closed her mouth.

His black brows met. 'Sit down. You look as though the wind could blow you away.'

Struggling with a shocking, unjust disappointment, she lowered herself into the elderly cane armchair. It took effort to arrange her hands loosely in her lap, and even more to say, 'I was going to write.' Perhaps it was a need for reassurance that compelled her to add, 'Would you have come even if you'd known I was pregnant?'

His scathing glance chilled her to the bone. 'I realise you don't have much of an opinion of me,' he said with biting precision, 'but what sort of man would I be to ignore my own child? One of these days you'll finally admit that I'm not like your stepfather.'

Although, she thought cynically, he'd been prepared to play James Sanderson at his own game. 'I know you're not.'

Perhaps she spoke too quickly, too carelessly, because his mouth compressed. Unable to meet his intent regard, she looked down. The adrenalin surge was fading fast, replaced by the leaden tiredness that had become her constant companion.

He waited, as though expecting her to continue; when she didn't he said crisply, 'It doesn't matter now—we have to decide what to do.'

'I suppose I want you to make it all better,' she said ironically. 'Stupid of me. But this is your child, too, and you do have rights.'

When she lifted her eyes she saw his gaze flick to her mouth, to her hair, and then, significantly, to her waist. 'Some women would disagree,' he said neutrally.

It was like trudging through a desert—there were no signposts, no ways of telling whether she was heading in the right direction. 'If you don't want anything to do with the baby I'll understand. I know you did your best to prevent one.'

'And obviously failed. That's not relevant.'

Angry with herself for needing something he wasn't able to give—and angry with him for playing his cards so close to his chest—she said, 'I want what's best for the baby.'

'What does that mean?' His eyes were hooded in his expressionless face.

She said shortly, 'It means a father—not live-in, but there for it. If you don't want that, then you can stay completely out of its life.'

Tension weighted the moment before he spoke. 'I want very much to be a part of my child's life, so I suggest we go back to New Zealand and get married.'

'Married?' The word sounded stupid, heavy. 'No!'

She must have gone pale because he walked across to the kitchen and poured a glass of water, bringing it to her. Their fingers touched, and the familiar desire scorched through her. She jerked away.

'Stop being coy. Touching me won't poison you,' he said caustically, and held the glass out with a rock-steady hand.

Carefully avoiding his fingers, she grasped the tumbler and lifted it to her mouth, hiding behind it while the cool water slid down her throat and her pulses throbbed erratically.

Keir said dispassionately, 'I know that nowadays it's almost normal to bear children in happy unwedlock, but marriage will give our baby a legal relationship with me.'

A nameless emotion ached through her. 'It's not necessary. It will complicate—'

'It will also give *you* a legal claim on me,' he broke in, his level, inflexible voice silencing her.

'I don't need that.' She drained the water. The roaring in her head had faded, but she could feel his implacable will beating at her.

Broad shoulders lifted in a shrug. Although he was wearing well-cut trousers and a fine cotton shirt, for a second she saw him as he'd been the night of the storm, perhaps the very night the baby was conceived, magnificent in his nudity, tanned skin gleaming in the stormlight. Her heart jumped and heat roiled inside her, tugging at her nerves, clouding her mind with fumes of remembered sensuality.

As calmly as though they were discussing a business deal, he said, 'I think you do. Can you say you trust me?' He waited while she looked away, thoughts churning fruitlessly, and smiled unpleasantly. 'No, I didn't think so. Marrying me will give you something legal to cling to. And I don't want our child to think its parents didn't care enough about it to formalise its relationship with both of them.'

Hope could feel him willing her to look up, but she kept her eyes on the ray of sunlight trapped and focused by the glass in her hand. 'I am not going to marry you,' she said thinly.

On a note of controlled impatience he said, 'There's also the gossip factor; because of what I am, who I am, journalists will nose around. Our names—and the child's—will be bandied around in the sort of headlines we've seen too often.'

Appalled, Hope clenched her hand on the glass. 'I hadn't thought of that,' she admitted, trying to marshal her thoughts into order. The infuriating, debilitating weariness weighed her down, slowing her responses—except, she thought irritably, the purely physical! She rallied enough to say firmly, 'We don't need to get married because your name will be on the birth certificate. That will give you a formal relationship to the baby. As for the gossip—who cares?'

Keir said uncompromisingly, 'You'll care when you can't go anywhere without having a camera poked in your face, when photographs of the child appear in the gutter press every time my name comes up in a business deal. If we're married you'll be sheltered from the worst of that.'

She felt her face settle into obstinate lines, and he added coolly, 'And having my name on the birth certificate is not enough.'

'I won't live a lie, play happy families,' she said with rapid, painful passion. 'Not even for the baby. My mother did that for my sake.' It took all of her strength to say bleakly and firmly, 'Stop harassing me, Keir. I'm not going to marry you.'

He didn't hesitate. 'Like you, I want what's best for our child. We're two adults—I'm sure we can come up with some sort of arrangement that will suit us both and make a happy life for the baby.'

When she refused to look at him his voice hardened. 'If you're afraid that I'll expect you to sleep with me, forget it. It's more than obvious that you don't want me to touch you.'

Of course a pregnant woman wasn't sexy—very poor lover or mistress material.

But she still wanted him; her body still sang when he touched her, her mind still turned to jelly. How could she keep her independence intact if she married him?

He said forcefully, 'This is not about sex, Hope. It's not about dominance, either. I'm not going to turn into another James Sanderson the minute I put a wedding ring on your finger.'

'I didn't—I know you wouldn't,' she said curtly.

His harsh, unamused laugh brought her head whipping round. He was still smiling, but his eyes were ice-cold as he said sardonically, 'Don't lie to me, Hope.' His face hardened. 'If we're going to make shared parenthood work, we need to build some sort of relationship for the sake of the baby—we can do that while we're waiting for its birth.'

He was right. Eventually this fierce physical hunger must die, and then she'd have some peace, but there would always be their child. Hiding the bitterness of surrender with a poker face, Hope said tonelessly, 'I am not going to marry you. Don't take it personally; I don't ever intend to marry anyone.'

Shivering, she got to her feet and walked over to the window. Beads of sweat popped out across her forehead, over her upper lip, between her breasts. She hugged herself tightly, rubbing her hands up suddenly cold arms. From a distance she heard his voice, harsh and then fading, and she crumpled.

She regained consciousness to hear him talking crisply, his deep voice biting out words she couldn't discern. She was lying down, and there was something deliciously cold and wet on her forehead.

As she forced her eyelids up he said, 'All right, I have to go.'

He'd been talking on his mobile telephone. Now he snapped it shut and came across the bedroom, sitting down on the side of the bed. 'Feeling better?' he asked quietly.

'Yes.'

She swallowed, and he lifted her up and held a glass of water for her. After she'd drunk the cool liquid he said, 'Don't worry. I didn't mean to upset you so much. Just relax.'

When his arms came around her she relaxed gratefully against him until common sense drove her to lift her head and pull away. 'Oh, I hate this,' she said in a husky voice, avoiding his eyes.

'Have you seen a doctor?'

'Yes, today.' Although her skin still wanted his touch, his closeness, she managed a smile. 'I told you before, it's part of the normal process of pregnancy. It should go by the second trimester.'

'Lie down,' he commanded, easing her back against the pillow.

For several seconds he looked at her, obviously weighing his next words. His eyes had spokes of darker grey radiating from the pupil; it was these that seemed to refract the light into crystalline splinters, making it impossible to see the man behind the mask of force and power. Sharp, fierce awareness needled through Hope, routing her exhaustion.

'I won't harass you any more,' he said at last. 'But I have to make sure you're all right. I'll hire a house here and we can move into it, at least until you're over this fainting.'

Closing her eyes, she breathed in and out several times, willing the heady fumes of sexual hunger to dissipate. They didn't, but she managed to grab the reins of her composure. 'What about your work?' she muttered.

Long, ruthless fingers tilted her chin. 'Look at me,' he commanded.

Slowly, reluctantly, her lashes lifted.

His eyes were grave, their transparent depths unrelenting as they scanned her face. 'You need someone to look after you and the baby, and that person should be me—we're in this together, Hope. If you won't marry me and come back to New Zealand, then I'll move here. It's as simple as that.'

Hope jerked her chin away. Living in the same house as Keir wasn't going to help her keep this obsession shackled and harmless, yet she sensed his ruthless determination to take care of her.

He got to his feet. 'You're worn out,' he said roughly. 'At least stay with me until you're able to function properly.'

Sighing, she yielded. 'All right, and I'll go with you back to New Zealand. It makes no sense for you to rearrange your whole life. But as soon as I feel better I'll make my own arrangements. I hate feeling like a wimp!'

His smile was ironic and uncompromising. 'A more stubborn, strong-minded wimp I've yet to come across. All right, that's decided. Let's get going.'

'Don't just charge ahead and expect me to follow meekly!'

He stooped and kissed her, not on the mouth but on the forehead, straightening before she'd had time to register much more than a fleeting masculine scent, and a subtle re-arrangement of something deep inside her.

'I'm not so stupid,' he said with something that sounded very like mockery in his deep voice.

Three hours later Hope stood at the window of the huge sitting room high in one of the hotels that bordered the beach. 'I am impressed,' she said lightly, 'with such forceful efficiency. From hovel to luxury in a few short hours.'

'Money helps,' he told her with cool pragmatism.

She looked down across the shaded sand and the broad turquoise expanse of the Coral Sea. Apprehension gripped her; the time spent in Keir's house would change her in ways she couldn't foresee.

Oh, grow up, she thought impatiently. Motherhood alters everything—that's why Keir's with you, why you're in his suite being pampered by a personal maid and butler, why you're flying to New Zealand tomorrow!

'Don't start worrying,' he said, reading her with the uncanny perceptiveness she resented. He crossed the ceramic-tiled floor and took her hand, holding it loosely yet firmly in his. 'We'll work things out.'

Why couldn't she be one of those women who bloomed when they were pregnant, whose minds stayed clear and alert? 'It's such a huge step,' she said, her voice charged with sombre resignation.

'Would you feel more secure if I got my solicitor to draw up an agreement, setting out exactly what I'll do for you and the child?'

A blunt refusal hovered on the tip of her tongue, but because her emotions were no longer trustworthy she made herself consider the idea. In spite of that cynical remark about his money, he was completely competent and organised; he'd made it so simple for her to pack up and leave with him.

Just occasionally, she thought grimly, it was nice to be coddled.

That was her hormones speaking—it had to be, because she'd never wanted anyone to care for her, never wanted to be caught in that trap.

'Perhaps an agreement would be a good idea,' she said. Driven by an old distrust, she added, 'And as the whole idea is to give the baby a stable background, we'll need to think carefully about how we're going to organise our lives around it.'

For a moment she thought she saw a look of cold determination in his face, but a second glance told her she'd been mistaken. His features were austere and expressionless.

'Have you had any thoughts on the terms of custody?'

'Shared,' she said instantly.

He gave her a keen look, then gave her a twisted smile. 'Thank you. You don't trust me to be a good husband, but you think I'll make a reasonable father.'

Although his words chilled her, that smile sank into her like a shaft of sunlight, warming some frozen part of her, sending her pulse-rate into the stratosphere. By a perverse trick of fate an image of Aline popped into her brain—elegant, sophisticated, eminently suitable. Rapidly, almost angrily, she said, 'They're not the same thing.'

Crystalline eyes probing and intent, he said in an unsettling tone, 'I'm glad you think so.'

A pink biplane chugged past, giving some fortunate tourists a slow view of the beach and the city centre, of the canals behind, of holidaymakers and residents and the steep-sided, blue-grey plateaux of the hinterland.

Keir asked in an equivocal tone, 'Why did you decide to sleep with me in Noosa?'

Startled and shocked, she firmed her mouth and met his level, measuring gaze with straight brows and an angled chin.

After a second of cowardly hesitation, she decided to stick with honesty, and to hell with his ego.

Making her tone rueful, her smile direct and a little mocking, she said, 'At eighteen, Keir, I put you on a pedestal along with Lancelot and Keanu Reeves. Unfortunately, I didn't grow out of it. When we met again I realised I was stuck in a time warp, forever a teenager yearning for a man she couldn't have. I wanted freedom, and it looked as though the only way I was going to get it was to give in to that obsession.'

As a cure it had been a conspicuous failure; she was still violently susceptible to his powerful masculine charisma, the exciting contrast of tanned skin and crystalline eyes and black hair, the way her hormones surged into overdrive when her gaze tangled with his.

'I see.'

She stayed where she was, praying that he wouldn't notice that her skin was on fire, that she had to clench her hands to stop them shaking, hold her shoulders and back straight.

'So you used me to scratch an itch.' His words burned, yet the tone was ice. 'What would you think of a man who did that to a woman, Hope? You'd say he exploited her.'

He was right. She swung around, her head high, her eyes glittering in her pale face. 'Any scruples I might have felt were shattered four years ago when I heard you agree to deal with my father. And you did cut a deal, didn't you, Keir? What did he offer—my sexual services in return for his security and the appearance of power? He'd have hated giving up control, but he must have accepted that you'd won—otherwise he wouldn't have suggested such a bargain.' She paused, scanning the dark, forbidding face. Deliberately she finished, 'How exasperating for you and unfortunate for him that my mother got me away before either of you could collect!'

CHAPTER NINE

IT GAVE Hope a tormented satisfaction to watch his expression freeze, his heavy lashes half hide those icy eyes, his mouth tighten into a thin line.

'Surely you remember?' she asked, driving home the point. 'The night before you left for America—the last time I saw you before I left New Zealand? I was on the balcony and I overheard most of the very interesting conversation you had with my father.'

A muscle flicking in his jaw, Keir demanded, 'What the hell were you doing out there?'

Her lips stretched in a painful, meaningless smile. 'I wanted to say goodbye because you were leaving early the next morning, but my father came in with you. When I heard him I panicked and scrambled through the French windows.'

The little tourist aeroplane chugged by again, but the room was filled with silence.

Harshly Keir broke it. 'How much did you hear?'

'I clapped my hands over my ears when you agreed to bargain with him.' She waited, then added, 'Just after you'd told him that you had only to whistle and I'd leap into your bed.'

Keir said something succinct and brutal under his breath.

In spite of the humiliation that crawled through her, Hope managed a shrug. 'It was a bit shattering, although I wasn't exactly surprised. I had spent quite a lot of time wondering why you courted me so assiduously.'

'Not, I assure you, so that I could seduce your father's ramshackle empire from him,' he said scathingly. He sat back and crossed his legs at the ankles, his half-closed eyes calculating. 'I'm sorry you overheard, but even sorrier you stopped listening right there. If you'd hung in any longer you'd have heard me threaten your father with immediate bankruptcy if I ever heard anything like that from him again.'

Hope was appalled at how much she wanted to believe him. But, starkly convincing, the scorn in his voice as he'd said he could have her any time he cared to snap his fingers rang down through the years.

Tension tightened every sinew, throbbed behind Hope's eyes. Flattening her tone in an effort to hide her pain, she retorted scornfully, 'You said, "What's in it for me?"' She drew in a ragged breath. 'And you said, "Let's deal." It certainly didn't sound as though you were upset—or even surprised—by his suggestion.'

'I was sickened that a man could be so depraved.' His voice was deep and inflexible, his expression uncompromising. 'I did not agree to his terms.' After a knife-blade glance at her strained face, he said bitingly, 'So when we met again you saw a perfect chance for revenge?'

She muttered in a tissue-thin voice, 'It wasn't revenge.' But had there been an element of paying him back in her decision?

'Then what was it? And don't give me any more rubbish about time warps or pedestals. You set out to make me suffer for what you saw as a betrayal.'

Goaded, she snapped, 'I set out to get you out of my system!'

'Did you indeed?' he said in a voice that chilled every cell in her body. 'Did it work?'

Hope's head jerked as though she'd been hit on the chin. He waited with intimidating courtesy, and when she refused to answer he finally said, 'When we met in Noosa, why didn't you ask me to explain what you'd overheard?'

She was surprised into a harsh laugh. 'I *heard* you, Keir, dealing with my father, bargaining, beating him down from marriage until he offered me as a mistress. *What is there to explain?'*

Anger clamped his features into a mask. 'I overreacted stupidly and arrogantly to a suggestion I found utterly distasteful. I tried to shame him into realising that he was acting as a pimp, trying to sell me a wife in part-payment of a debt.'

When she didn't reply he said in a voice honed to a sharp edge of contempt, 'You thought you were in love with me, yet you believed that I'd bargain for you, trade you like a parcel of shares? I don't call that love! I was so angry I had to stop myself from hitting him.'

'I wish you had,' she returned cordially, hoping her tone didn't reveal how carefully she was choosing her words. 'But if you were so disgusted, why did you suggest a deal?'

'To find out how rattled he was.' His face was sardonic, a cold mask that showed no mercy. 'When he offered you as a sweetener I knew he was desperate and that I'd won.'

Smiling with acid derision, Hope said, 'Why didn't *you* tell me this when we met again? I gave you plenty of opportunities.'

'I'm not a mind-reader,' he returned caustically. 'I didn't know you'd eavesdropped on a private conversation, so I failed entirely to pick up the clues. As for telling you—not only do you believe that I'd accept such an infamous bargain, but you think I'd hurt and humiliate you with the sordid details of your stepfather's behaviour!' Grimly derisive, he finished, 'You don't think much of me, do you, Hope?'

His tone stung like a whiplash. Although everything in her longed to believe that he was incapable of betraying her, she said in a soft, bitter tone, 'Even then I knew that a man like you couldn't be interested in a girl straight from school.'

'You had no idea what sort of man I was,' Keir told her contemptuously.

'I found out.' She went on with judicious insolence, 'Ambitious, ruthless, charming, sexy—far too much for me to handle. So why *did* you ask me out, Keir, if it wasn't to keep an eye on my father?'

'I asked you out because you were the most enchanting girl I'd ever met.' A dark emotion licked beneath the words, like flames running along a seam of coal deep underground.

Hope flinched, a violent longing hammering through her. A yacht slipped around the end of a peninsula and headed south, white sails gleaming in the sunlight, an image of freedom.

'Enchanting—and far too young.' His voice was coldly cynical. 'In Noosa I thought you'd grown up, but I was wrong. You're still locked in the past.'

Switching her gaze from the beach and the limitless stretch of ultramarine sea to the marble and raw silk opulence of the suite, Hope winced at the energy and determination in his dangerous face.

She had been such a fool! What she'd misread as desperation to exorcise an old passion had been desire's treacherous bait. Now they were both imprisoned in a trap fashioned of duty and obligation.

'Perhaps,' she admitted, fighting a wave of exhaustion. 'I know I behaved stupidly. Offering you a relationship when I'm not able to sustain one.' He didn't respond, and eventually she muttered, 'I'm sorry.'

Keir got up and took a step towards her, then stopped as she backed away. In a voice that was detached and steady he said, 'We've both made mistakes. Now that we're aware of them, surely we can leave them behind, put the past where it belongs.'

'You can never leave the past behind,' she said, suddenly empty of all emotion. 'It doesn't matter, anyway. You're right—what's done is done, and the baby is more important than my poor, smarting, little adolescent heart. I know this whole situation must be a huge nuisance for you, but we'll have to make the best of it.'

He scanned her face. 'You're exhausted,' he said roughly. 'Go and lie down. I'll have a meal sent up and you can eat it in bed.'

'I'm not sick,' she said with automatic defensiveness.

A glitter in his smile warned her that he'd reached the end of his patience. 'Humour me,' he said between his teeth, and when she still didn't move he picked her up and carried her into the bedroom.

Hope stiffened in the strong, protective cage of his arms. 'I do dislike men who use their strength against women,' she said in a voice she strove to hold steady against the thunder of her pulses and the fireflow of sensation gathering deep in the pit of her stomach.

'You were swaying on your feet,' he said without apology, and deposited her on the huge bed. This time his smile was laced with a rueful charm that stabbed her in the heart. 'Stop fighting me, Hope. It can't be good for you, and I'm sure it's not good for the baby. Relax. And try to believe that I'm nothing like James Sanderson.'

She watched him go, appalled at her need to believe him. In too many ways he reminded her of the man who'd used her as a bargaining tool.

Yet her father had been arrogant and arbitrary, victim of a pathological need to control, whereas Keir's natural authority was disciplined and directed by his intelligence.

He was certainly strong-willed, she thought as she stood up and walked into the bathroom, but there was a difference between Keir's hard integrity and her father's lust to dominate.

Her heart told her that Keir was incapable of the sort of ritual humiliation forced on her mother. She frowned solemnly at her reflection, admitting that, although she longed to, she dared not trust her judgement, clouded as it was by this obsessive passion she didn't seem to be able to sate or dismiss.

*   *   *

Hope had expected it to be raining when they arrived in Auckland; however, the sleek private jet flew in over a city lit by the sun, its two harbours gleaming like beaten silver surrounded by farmlands of glowing, vivid green, the suburbs bright-roofed and fresh beneath a canopy of trees.

'I'd forgotten how lovely it is,' she said quietly.

Keir lifted an eyebrow. 'It's one of the most beautiful settings in the world.'

'I know.' Her voice trailed off. Perhaps today's sun was an omen...

Or perhaps not. Keir had retreated behind a façade of impeccable politeness and reserve. She'd followed suit, so they'd been moving around each other with the meticulous care and watchfulness of two duellers in a bout to the death.

There were distinct advantages to being the companion of a very rich man. Travelling with Keir was comfortable and efficient and quick. After a speedy trip through Customs a car met them, long and luxurious; the driver loaded the luggage in the boot while Keir put Hope into the front seat.

'All right?' he asked with one penetrating glance at her.

'Yes, thank you.'

A few minutes later they were heading north on the motorway. 'Do you drive?' he asked.

Hope nodded, covering a small yawn with her hand.

'Do you have any preferences for a make of car?'

She closed her mouth so firmly her teeth clicked. 'You don't need to buy me a car.'

'Without one you'll be stuck at home all day.' He accelerated to pass a truck. 'Even if you don't drive to Auckland you'll want to go into the village occasionally, and I won't always be there to take you.'

Fretfully she muttered, 'I don't expect anyone to chauffeur me around.'

'I'll see about a car. You'll need a safe one, suitable for a baby.'

Hope nodded. 'Of course,' she said, wondering why she felt so—empty.

He gave her a swift, narrow glance. 'Sleep if you want to. It will take us forty minutes or so to get home.'

Now that she could give in to the tiredness, she didn't feel like sleeping. To fill the silence, she asked, 'How often do you travel for business?'

'About a week or so out of every month. Sometimes more, sometimes less.'

Those weeks away would be much-needed respites for her. Her vulnerability scared her—she didn't want to depend on this man, yet once he'd turned up again she'd agreed to almost everything he'd decided. And pregnancy was no excuse, even though her mind had turned to mush and her energy had seeped away.

'Tell me about your work,' she said.

'It's work,' he said. 'Fascinating to me, but not of much interest to anyone else.'

'That sounds,' she said mildly, not attempting to hide the thread of steel through her words, 'as though you think I should mind my own business.'

'I don't want to bore you.'

'I don't bore easily.' It was impossible, she thought with a clutch of panic, to imagine being bored by Keir.

His shoulders lifting in a slight shrug, he began to talk about people he'd met, situations he'd found himself in. As befitted a banker he was discreet—no names and in some cases not even places—but he told a good story, using dry wit and a sharp turn of phrase to render the people and occasions vivid and memorable.

Hope was laughing about a hectic experience in South America involving gauchos, interminable barbecues, and an attempt to throw a weapon consisting of balls suspended from cords, when he turned the wheel and the car left the main highway and ducked down a narrow gravel road. Her amusement died, leaving her cold and apprehensive. She pulled her upper lip between her teeth, then released it, looking straight ahead.

About ten minutes later Keir nodded to the left. 'There's Te Matataa.'

Hope drew a deep sighing breath. The road had twisted along a spine of hills that sloped down to a wide valley. On a low rise above the valley floor stood a proud Victorian house, serene and gracious. Double-storeyed, its verandahs embellished with wooden lace, it stood in wide lawns surrounded by huge, old trees.

Cattle lifted their heads as the car purred past them on a sealed drive, then went back to grazing in paddocks so green they made her blink. The gullies were thick with second-growth bush.

'You can see Auckland on the horizon,' Hope said wonderingly, 'yet this looks a million miles away.'

'It feels like it, too.' Keir drove over a cattle-stop. In a voice that was easy and pleasant he went on, 'If you're not happy here there's an apartment in Auckland, or I'll buy you a house wherever you want.'

'I'll be fine,' Hope said quietly.

'I want to know if you aren't.' It wasn't a question. Although he tempered the tone of his voice, she was abruptly and unpleasantly reminded that this man ran a huge organisation.

In Noosa she'd almost been able to forget Keir Carmichael, billionaire; he'd simply been the man she'd once loved. Being whisked back to New Zealand forced her to accept that she was carrying the child of a man who wielded vast power—and accepted the equally vast responsibility that went with it.

For a moment her heart quailed; stiffening her backbone, she smiled and said firmly, 'You should know me well enough by now to realise that I'll complain loudly and frequently.'

'Good.' The car came to a halt beside another, smaller one beside the front steps.

Keir unclipped his seatbelt and leaned towards her. Hope froze, ensnared by the polished clarity of his gaze. With a sudden feral urgency he lifted her chin and kissed her.

'Welcome home,' he murmured, his voice slightly thickened, and kissed her again until she shivered with a sensual languor that turned her eyes slumbrous and her mouth soft and tender.

When he lifted his head she whispered in a strangled voice, 'We decided we wouldn't—'

'There's no reason for anyone to know that we're not normal lovers,' he said in a cool, deliberate tone, and opened the car door.

How strange that he should need to appease some inner demon by making sure that no one suspected their relationship to be a farce.

They were met at the front door by a thin woman with unlikely red hair who said briskly, 'Hello, Keir. You have a visitor.' Her lack of expression indicated an equal lack of welcome.

For a moment Hope thought that the housekeeper was referring to her, and her heart sank.

Keir ignored a shadowy figure behind the older woman and said, 'Maria, this is Hope Sanderson.' All potent male charisma, intent and sexual, he smiled at Hope.

Hope held out her hand and after a moment's hesitation it was taken. As they shook hands the person behind the housekeeper said serenely, 'Keir, it's about time you came home. All hell is breaking out in the stockmarkets.'

The moment Hope heard the creamy, feminine, alert voice, she bristled. What was Aline doing here—did she make a habit of ambushing Keir in his own house? Then realisation struck. Of course, Keir had recognised the car and reacted with ruthless speed, kissing Hope stupid.

He said calmly, 'Aline, you know Hope, of course.'

Hope said, 'Hello.'

Her compassion was tested when Aline gave her a swift, dismissive smile. 'Visiting New Zealand for a while, Hope?'

'Hope is staying with me,' Keir interposed, his tone perfectly pleasant if you discounted the flinty undernote.

With another smile, Aline murmured, 'Do enjoy your visit.' Her tone just stopped short of insinuating *while you can*.

'I plan to make sure she does,' Keir said.

Aline's patrician face went blank before lightening in a pretty laugh. 'Oh, dear, and I have to interrupt your homecoming with business! I'm afraid it won't wait, Keir; we have a problem that's going to get much, much worse overnight if we don't tackle it immediately.'

The panelled hall was huge and rather dark, with an ornate flight of stairs rising to the second storey. Hope felt disconnected, almost disassociated, as though she inhabited a different reality. The familiar scent of lavender and beeswax reminded her poignantly of her grandmother's home.

From outside the wide front door came the housekeeper's voice, busy directing someone called Johnno to take care with the bags.

Keir took Hope's elbow. 'All right,' he said pleasantly, 'I'll see you in the office in a few minutes.'

With a smile that cooled as it travelled from Keir to Hope, Aline said, 'Yes, of course,' and turned to walk away from them, her back and shoulders erect.

Again Hope felt an unwilling stab of compassion.

Keir waited until they'd reached the top of the stairs before saying, 'I'm sorry about that.' He pushed a door open.

'I'm sorry for *her*.' To give herself something to do, Hope looked around the bedroom.

'Even when she was as rude to you as she dared to be?'

Startled, she looked up, meeting eyes as cold and clear as a frosty night. Furious because a stark twist of jealousy overrode her sympathy for Aline's personal tragedy, she snapped, 'Did you see her face?'

'Yes,' he said briefly. 'I know you want some explanation—'

'It's none of my business,' Hope interrupted.

He paused—it was impossible to think of Keir hesitating— then said deliberately, 'Even if I loved her—and I don't— I'd want a real, live woman in my life, not one who's determined to remain another man's widow in all the most important ways.'

No wonder he'd done his best to persuade her to marry him; marriage—any sort of marriage—would be his best shield against Aline's determination. Hope swallowed words that had suddenly developed thorns and nodded.

A warm light from the windows picked out the thrusting, arrogantly defined framework of his face, the width of his shoulders, the lean, sinewy strength and beauty of his hands. Hope's heart turned over. Aline might still be in love with her dead husband, but she'd have to be dead herself not to respond to Keir's male potency!

'Don't worry about her,' Keir said abruptly. Frowning, he looked around the large room with its heavily draped French windows opening out onto a wooden verandah. 'I'd forgotten how old-fashioned this is. Do you want to check out the other bedrooms? You might feel more comfortable in one of them.'

'This is lovely.' Because neither words nor voice sounded enthusiastic, she added with more force, 'Thank you.'

Mouth tightening, he gave her a glinting look. 'Do something for me.'

'What?'

'Stop thanking me,' he said with a raw, barely suppressed violence that took her completely by surprise.

Her stomach clenching unpleasantly, she nodded.

He said, 'Do you want someone to unpack for you?'

'No.' The word almost exploded into the quiet air, sounding naked without the conventional thanks. Deliberately, Hope tacked on, 'I've told you over and over that I'm not sick.'

His brows snapped together, but he nodded and left without saying any more.

Hope sank down on the bed and stared sightlessly at a pretty watercolour on the wall, its amateur status proclaimed by shaky perspective. She knew that this house had been in Keir's family for five generations; it spoke of a settled, stable life.

The walls clamped around her, stifling her. She jumped at a sharp knock, then took in three deep breaths and opened the door. Keir strode in with her luggage.

'All right?' he said, dumping the pack onto a convenient stool and setting the box containing her computer on the floor beside it.

Hope gave him a hard look. 'I'll stop thanking you if you stop asking me if I'm all right,' she said crisply.

It was impossible to tell what he was thinking, but that rare smile broke through, swamping her in charm. 'It's a deal.'

His choice of words—deliberate, she realised as her eyes met his challenging ones—eased a little of the bitterness she'd been harbouring for the past four years. For a moment she hesitated, then held out her hand. 'It's a deal,' she agreed.

His grip was strong and sure and warm, and as she unpacked she wondered if it had lingered a little longer than necessary.

Half an hour later Hope closed the dressing room door on the last of her clothes. They looked as out of place as her small selection of cosmetics and toiletries in the opulent bathroom with its sophisticated Art Deco fittings.

This lovely old homestead was made for elegant, expensive, exclusive people, not a newly pregnant woman who'd learned to make economy an art form.

Confidence lurching dangerously, she looked out of the window. Both cars had gone. Setting her jaw, she emerged from the sanctuary of the bedroom, almost tiptoeing along the corridor.

'Oh, for heaven's sake!' she muttered, setting her heels down firmly.

But it took a considerable amount of courage to walk down the stairs. Once in the hall, she gazed around at the collection made by various members of Keir's family—photographs, some dimly painted heraldic shields, a splendid set of shelves displaying china, its mellow colours and charming designs hinting at a great age.

When the hair on her neck lifted she swung around, and there was Keir with a tray. 'My great-grandmother's pride and joy,' he said with a probing look. 'Come into the morning room and have something to drink.'

Once inside the comfortably shabby room she said, 'I can't drink coffee any more. For the past couple of weeks even the smell has made my stomach lurch.'

'I'll take it back to the kitchen.' He left before she could protest. Hope hesitated, then walked across to the window, staring out at green lawns and formal borders.

'Sit down,' Keir commanded from behind her, 'and pour.'

After a speaking glance—one he parried with raised brows and an unsparing smile—she obeyed, filling in the intimidating silence with a couple of banal comments about the house.

He accepted the cup she handed him and held it, long fingers relaxed, as she poured tea for herself and added milk.

Her hands were *not* relaxed; she held the cup and saucer too tightly.

To cover the tell-tale clattering of china against china, she asked, 'What can I do to help while I'm here?' The words sounded foreign and very lame so she hurried on, 'You might as well make the most of me. If you want me to…well, to give dinner parties or things, I can do that.'

His expression didn't alter, and yet she got a sudden, unexpected intimation of extreme anger. Her gaze flew upwards, registered a mask-like face, disciplined to reveal no emotion as he drawled, 'Can you?'

A primitive warning prickled through her. 'I'm actually a good cook—'

'So is Maria,' he said negligently, 'and I don't do much entertaining here. But if you want to invite friends, do so.'

Rebuffed, she snapped, 'Thank you—you're very kind.'

Keir picked up his cup and drank, pale eyes veiled by black lashes while Hope wondered edgily what had caused the crackling tension of the past few moments.

'I'm not kind,' he said evenly; then, as though the remark meant nothing, he asked about her exploits since she'd last been in New Zealand

With spirited determination she followed his lead. 'I've driven a bulldozer in an opencast mine and organised a reunion for a family of five hundred. And I was kitchenmaid and part-time cook and general skivvy in a very upmarket bed-and-breakfast establishment on the border between England and Scotland.'

Keir's angular face relaxed into amusement. She added dulcetly, 'Also, I can do a brilliant manicure. Any time you want inch-long acrylic nails with fake diamonds embedded in them, you just let me know.'

'A versatile woman,' he drawled. 'You'd be extremely useful on the farm—a wife who can drive a bulldozer is what every landowner wants. Not to mention your talent with fingernails.' Did he anticipate some sort of shared life after the baby was born? No, of course not.

Because her heart leapt at that prospect, she responded curtly, 'I won't be here then.' She paused, then added, 'I'll have to find something to do—something I can make a career of.'

'Such as?'

'I don't know yet,' she said with determination, 'but I'm going to find out. Writing, perhaps. I'm good at travel writing—I've had quite a few articles accepted. I won't be able to travel with the baby, but I've drifted long enough, and I need to be a good role model for him or her.'

Keir's brows lifted. 'If you find life here a little slow you could redecorate the homestead.'

Startled, Hope looked up. 'I don't know anything about decorating.'

'It's a project like any other. You wear your clothes with flair and an innate skill for colour and style—I don't think you'd have any problems.' His glinting glance drifted from the subtle golds and ambers of her shirt to the darker trousers that hid her long legs, stirring her hormones into swift, passionate urgency. 'And from what you've just told me you can turn your hand to anything. Redecorating a house shouldn't be any harder than organising a family reunion or selling a travel article.' He delivered the challenge with the smooth efficiency of a knife slicing through silk.

'Keir, this is ridiculous—you'd need to be an expert to do justice to this place.'

'You can hire the expertise,' he said lazily. 'I've been putting it off because my grandfather loved the house the way it is, and it's comfortable. However, it was last redecorated in the days when servants did the work, and a complete revamp of the kitchen and laundry area would make things much easier for Maria.'

Hope put her cup and saucer down with a small crash. 'Does she want the place altered?'

'She started working for my grandfather the day she left school, and she's contented enough, but she's not getting any younger. If you feel like doing it I'd be grateful.' He got to his feet. 'You don't have to make up your mind now, but I know you—if you're stuck here with nothing to do you'll go stir-crazy. Good, you've finished your tea. I have some papers in my office that you need to look at.'

In the office he handed her a document from the top of a small pile.

Making sure she didn't touch his fingers, Hope stared at the writing. 'It didn't take you long to set this up,' she said gruffly.

'I keep a solicitor on retainer,' he told her impersonally. 'Read it carefully and if there's anything you dislike let me know. I've organised for you to see an independent solicitor who'll look after your interests.'

Frowning, an odd chill pooling through her, she read the draft copy of the agreement.

Keir would pay all expenses for the child or children of their union until such time as it or they were in gainful employment. Further, he'd buy Hope a house, and pay her a substantial amount annually until she was able to earn her own living. The figure danced crazily in front of Hope's astonished eyes. Huskily she said, 'That's far too much.'

'We can negotiate,' he said on an uncompromising note that made a mockery of his suggestion, 'but you are the mother of my child. Any income I settle on you is rightfully yours.'

'I feel as though you're buying me off,' she said tightly.

His brows rose. With cool, forbidding arrogance he said, 'If you were the sort of woman I could buy off you wouldn't be here, and I'd be demanding DNA tests.'

When the words settled down, she read that unless a court

ruled otherwise they'd share custody of any child or children of their union.

'Children?' she asked.

He met her eyes with a bland look. 'Lawyers always want everything dotted and crossed.'

She cleared her throat. 'It looks pretty straightforward.' The document dropped with a slithering rustle onto the polished wooden surface of the desk.

Keir said, 'Good. Feel free to amend it. Would you like to go out to dinner tonight? I know an excellent restaurant not too far away, so unless you're too tired we could go there.'

She flicked him a doubtful glance. Remote, harsh, his face was shuttered against her. The excuse he'd offered hovered on her lips, but pride forbade her to take the easy way out. The prospect of spending an evening in the house facing his armour of well-polished politeness was not inspiring, especially as she was so aware of him her body was sizzling. And the alternative, retiring to a lonely bed, dismayed her. 'I'm not tired now,' she told him, and to her surprise it was true.

Broad shoulders moved slightly. 'Our child will be less of a shock to both the media and our friends if we're seen out together occasionally before it arrives.'

She wasn't the only one with pride; Keir was going to a lot of trouble to dampen down any publicity that came their way. Not surprising—what man would want the world to know that he'd been caught in the oldest trap of all, the baby trap?

'Then we'll go out to dinner,' she said, with a touch of arrogance all her own.

CHAPTER TEN

'MARIA, if I don't do something I'll go stark, staring crazy!' Hope glared belligerently at the housekeeper, who had just snatched the business end of the vacuum cleaner away from her. 'I've been here a whole month, pampered and waited on and barely allowed to move without someone checking on me, but I'm fine now. In fact, I'm just about bursting out of my skin with energy.'

Although Maria grinned sympathetically, she kept a firm hold of the vacuum cleaner as she switched it off. 'Keir told me to make sure you didn't overdo things, and around here we're in the habit of doing what Keir says.' With her free hand she made shooing motions at Hope. 'Go and sit in the conservatory; the mail's here, so you can read the paper and I'll bring you some tea. Once Keir comes home and gives you the OK you can start droving cattle for all I care.'

'Don't try and convince me you're afraid of him,' Hope grumbled, giving way.

Maria laughed. 'Of course I'm not, but Keir never does anything without a good reason. If he says you're not to do anything, he means it.'

He'd been in Europe a fortnight—with Aline—and Hope had missed him so much she sometimes thought she could taste it. Resigned, she turned towards the kitchen. 'All right, but I'll make the tea. Do you want a cup?'

'No, thanks, not just now.'

Once Hope had read the newspaper and drunk the tea, she sat back in the big chair and looked out across the garden, green and colourful under the golden swathe of the sun.

Spring was burgeoning with daffodils and the pretty

Englishness of annuals; a magnolia held huge pink cups up to the sky, each one splotched with crimson at the base. Keir was due back in three days, and she didn't know how she was going to cope. It had been bad enough before, when she'd been so tired, but now that her energy had poured back it was going to be sheer hell ignoring his powerful male magnetism.

And it was entirely her fault; she'd set the boundaries for their relationship, and he'd followed her lead. Since he'd known about the baby he'd treated her with exquisite, blood-less courtesy. They were very careful to be polite to each other, to discuss things like civilised people and keep their emotions firmly leashed.

Even when she'd been exhausted she'd wanted him with a primal passion. Now, she thought despairingly, her hands longed for the feel of black, thick, wavy hair, and she hun-gered to kiss him, to shiver at his deep voice, to climax to the driving, potent thrust of his body as he took her into that rapturous region that was theirs alone.

When it came to sex he understood her secret, unspoken needs and desires, and fulfilled her completely with his un-tamed male energy.

It would be perilously easy to become addicted. A shiver crawled across her skin; for the sake of her soul she had to resist.

'I wish life was simpler,' she muttered beneath her breath, unconsciously touching her waist where the child they'd made lay nested.

The afternoon dragged; Hope ate an early dinner, took a long luxurious bath, and got into bed with a favourite book.

When she sensed another presence she had to drag herself out of a dream. Lifting weighted eyelids, she mumbled, 'Keir?'

'Yes, it's Keir.'

His deep, slightly slurred voice summoned a swift upwelling of emotion. 'Oh,' she said, smiling into his dark features, 'you're home. Good.'

His face tightened. 'Is everything all right?'

'Yes,' she said drowsily, responding to his presence with involuntary delight. 'I missed you. How did it go?'

He laughed beneath his breath. 'Well enough, but I missed you, too.'

Hope held out her hand, and after a moment he took it and sat down on the side of the bed. His long fingers smoothed across hers, sending her pulses soaring. 'Maria says you've been driving her crazy this last week.'

It was so sweet to know he was back, to feel the strong warm clasp of his hand around hers. 'I've stopped languishing like a lily,' Hope said, smiling sleepily at him. 'I feel so good I just might redecorate the whole house while you're not looking. But I'll settle for you calling Maria off. Every time I take a breath deeper than normal she's there, terrified I'm going to exhaust myself.'

'I told her to make sure you didn't overdo things.' But his voice was abstracted, as though he was thinking of something else.

Hope's sideways glance followed his to their linked hands, dark skin against fine-grained ivory, blunt male power against delicate female strength. His face intent and absorbed, Keir stroked across her palm, then looped her wrist, his fingertips resting against the primitive drumbeat of her pulse. Hope's breath came rapidly between her lips; a mixture of fire and honey overwhelmed her, its source Keir's potent touch, his presence, the elusive, provocative body scent that was his alone.

He was aroused, she realised with abrupt urgency, and so was she, her body clamorous and seeking. He lifted her hand and kissed it, his mouth lingering on the blue veins at her wrist before moving to her palm. Sensation fired her nerves, ran like lightning through her, white-hot, consuming her with its forbidden lure.

'Keir...' she sighed, holding out her other hand in a gesture he couldn't mistake.

He paused before saying deeply, 'Are you sure?'

'I don't think I've ever been more sure of anything,' she said with stark honesty, accepting at last that she loved this man—had always loved him. And it wasn't going to go away.

If all he had to give her was his passion then she'd accept that, not ask for more.

He was still looking at her hand, his thick, straight black lashes like fans against his strong cheekbones. Her heart swelled; when he glanced up suddenly her breath stopped in her throat as she met the full blast of his desire, the molten hunger he didn't try to hide.

'I spent most of the time away thinking of you,' he said, his voice harsh. 'Longing for you, wanting you, wondering how you were. Talking to you on the telephone every night only fed my dreams.'

'But now you're home,' she said, her voice creamy with anticipation.

He kissed her then, and when that long draining kiss was over said on her lips, 'I love the way you say my name.'

'Keir,' she whispered, giving him the surrender he wanted.

And as they kissed again she thought dazedly that she wanted this, too, this long, bitterly fought surrender to love.

He made love to her with heart-shaking tenderness, with a passion that would echo through her for ever. Although as intense as their previous lovemakings, instead of the elemental urgency that had driven them before this time was marked by a slow, consuming sweetness.

'You are so beautiful,' he said unsteadily when he'd finished stripping her nightshirt from her. 'Honey skin, and honey-coloured hair, and eyes of rich, dark amber. When we make love it's like sinking into sweetness and fire and lightning…'

He spread her hair out on the pillow, then drew heavy tresses across her throat and kissed her through it.

'And skin like silk,' he said, cupping a breast that was heavy and charged with need. 'Smooth and fine and hot.'

He explored her body with hands and lips until she was panting with need, desperate for him. She tried her own particular punishment for that, and although his face grew stark and compelling she couldn't break his control. Still he caressed her with an exquisite gentleness that shuddered through her.

'Now,' she pleaded at last, so acutely conscious of him that she thought she would carry his image engraved on her brain for all time—sleek, tanned skin gleaming in the light, the long swell of muscle and the play of hair across his chest, down his flanks, and above it all the stark impression of force and power.

'Yes, now,' he said in his throat, and eased into her, rocking slowly, tormenting her with his single-minded restraint.

She made a soft, moaning noise in the back of her throat and rose to meet him, to claim him, to make him part of her.

But although he accepted that wordless challenge he refused to unleash his passion, taking her as though she was a virgin and for them both this was the first time. Lost in tenderness, she crested almost immediately, calling out wordlessly in the quiet old-fashioned room as the sweetness turned to a rage of surrender, followed immediately by the primitive fever of ecstasy. He came with her, yet even in his climax his passion was curbed, transmuted into gentleness.

Afterwards he held her until she slept, but when she woke late the next morning he'd been called away to Auckland, and she was left to roam the house with a heavy feeling of foreboding.

Late in the morning she found out what that knot in her

stomach portended. She was walking through the rose garden some previous Carmichael had constructed, imagining the transformation summer would make to these ruthlessly pruned bushes, when a movement from the verandah caught her eye.

Aline, she thought, watching the tall, slender woman walk gracefully and purposefully towards her. 'Hello,' she said with a smile she had to work really hard on.

Aline ignored it, and said with a curled lip, 'So you tried to trap Keir by getting pregnant. How trite and silly and common of you. I hope you don't think he'll marry you. He's a very responsible man, but he's not an idiot.'

'My relationship with Keir is none of your business,' Hope returned shortly, unable to respond as vigorously as she wanted to because something about the other woman's face revealed a kind of sick desolation.

'Why not? We are—were—lovers.'

Even as Hope tried to deflect the impact of those curt words, she recognised the truth in the other woman's eyes. Pain almost felled her, slamming into her with massive force. She wondered dimly if she was going to faint, but an inner strength born of pride kept her upright.

'And we will be again, when he's done his duty by you,' Aline said calmly. 'I can give him much more than you ever will.'

Oddly enough, the other woman's voice and words, her attitude, eased something deep inside Hope. With relief, she accepted at last that Aline didn't love Keir—would never love him.

'Why are you so determined to marry him when you're not in love with him?' Hope asked, her voice oddly brisk and flat. 'Don't you think he deserves to be loved as you loved your husband?'

Aline's beautiful face froze. 'Leave my husband out of this,' she spat.

'You apparently feel free to comment on my life and my relationships; I'm merely claiming the same right.'

'It's easy to see you're James Sanderson's daughter,' Aline sneered. 'You learned that vulgarity from him.'

Hope's head jerked but she answered calmly, 'He's my stepfather, not my father.'

Aline turned her head and contemplated a small bush, subdued by the pruner's merciless skill to mere sticks. When she looked back her face was wiped of expression. 'I didn't mean to turn this into a cat-fight. And I'm sorry that you think you're in love with him. I don't suppose it's any consolation, but you're not the only one. He has a fatal attraction.'

Hope didn't answer, and after a few seconds Aline resumed, 'However, you should realise that you have no future with Keir. Oh, he'll care for his child; he's a good man, with a strongly developed sense of responsibility, so you'll never have to worry about money or support, but that's all.'

'You seem to have no problems accepting that this is Keir's child,' Hope said, finding her way. Aline seemed so confident...

A faint, knowing smile crossed the older woman's lovely face. 'Keir will make sure it's his,' she said. 'I don't expect you to understand our relationship, but I can assure you that it's strong enough to withstand this complication. I probably won't be seeing much of you again, so I hope that everything goes well for you and the baby.' She nodded regally and turned away, walking through the formal beds back to the house.

Hope discovered that she was trembling. After a moment's thought she realised that it was with fury. And not because Aline had taken it upon herself to force this confrontation, but because Keir had made love to her. A fierce, hot jealousy drove all sensible thought from her head; she had to wrestle with her demons in the sun until the heat drove her inside.

'Did Ms Connors find you?' Maria asked, popping her head around the drawing room door.

'Yes, thank you.'

Hope thought she'd managed to keep an impassive face and level voice, but Marie's eyes widened a moment. 'Everything all right?' she asked neutrally.

'Yes.' Hope strode upstairs, coming to an abrupt halt in the middle of her bedroom. 'I can't *bear* it,' she said between clenched teeth.

Last night in that bed she'd finally acknowledged her love for Keir—and now this, the greatest betrayal of all! How dared he make love with Aline? But for some stupid reason the biggest sin was that he'd told her about the baby.

Half an hour later she was still stewing in the room, pacing recklessly back and forth. Her spine stiffened at a tap on the door. She swallowed and turned to face it. 'Come in,' she called, steadying her voice.

Keir walked in, tall and dark and dominant, still dressed in the dark business suit that made the most of his long legs and wide shoulders.

Hope's pulse-rate pushed through the ceiling. 'You're back early,' she said in a low, dangerous tone.

Ice-pale eyes surveyed her face. 'Maria called me,' he said laconically. 'She thought you looked pale and upset. What did Aline say to you?'

'That you were lovers,' she flashed back. 'No, to be a hundred per cent accurate, that you have been lovers and will be again when this complication—' her hand rested protectively on her waist '—is over.'

'And you believed her?'

She said bleakly, 'I saw the truth in her eyes. And I can see it in yours now.'

Keir swore, his deep voice raw with anger and frustration. 'We made love once,' he said with cold precision, watching her with hooded eyes. 'Once, months ago. It was stupid and unkind of me, and I regretted it the moment we'd done it.'

'Why didn't you tell me?'

His mouth hardened. 'Because it wasn't relevant. One night does not constitute an affair—we both agreed that it wasn't something we wanted to repeat.'

'Is that when she decided to marry you?'

Keir frowned. With reluctance he said aloofly, 'I suspect it was. I'm sorry it happened, and I have made it clear to her that it was an isolated incident. Why is it so important to you?'

She floundered for a moment before retorting, 'If I'd known it would have saved me some embarrassing moments.'

'You're more than capable of dealing with embarrassing moments,' he said, his judicial voice scraping across her sensitive nerves. 'You're a confident, capable, sensible woman, so why have you reverted right back to that eighteen-year-old girl who overheard her stepfather trying to barter her off so he could huddle the miserable vestiges of his power around him?'

'I haven't!' Stung, she lifted her chin. 'I'm not accustomed to being—dismissed—' She fell silent.

'She made you feel like a pawn, worth nothing.' His anger shimmered around him. Mercilessly he bored back in. 'You're feeling betrayed.' He waited while she stared at him, and then jerked her face sideways. In a tone compounded of ice and disgust he said, 'I can understand that, and I'm sorry. Perhaps I should have told you that I'd slept with Aline, but you didn't seem interested in anything else about me but my prowess as a lover.'

Hearing her own lies delivered back to her in that excoriating tone made Hope flinch.

Very quietly, very lethally, he said, 'I'm not promiscuous,

but I have made love to other women besides Aline—do you want a list?'

Heat surged up through her skin, heat and shame and that harsh anger. 'No,' she said angrily.

'I won't crawl across broken glass to prove over and over again that I'm not like your stepfather. You have to decide whether to trust me.'

A bitter smile twisted her mouth. 'Ah, that's the problem. I think I might love you—but I can't trust you.'

Panic kicked her hard beneath her breasts. How the hell had that slipped out? Her gaze flew to his ruthless face, set in mask of cold, unyielding disbelief.

He said cruelly, 'You don't know how to love. Love *is* trust.'

Hope shook her head, striving hard to quell the black fear that almost engulfed her. 'Why did you tell her I was pregnant?'

He said calmly, 'I didn't.'

'Then how did she know?' she demanded.

'I have no idea.' Keir's black brows drew together. 'Perhaps she noticed the difference, as I did—you look riper, yet more contained, as though you're drawing into yourself, preparing yourself—' His voice altered as she winced. 'What's the matter?'

'Nothing,' she said blankly. A twist of pain surfaced beneath her fingers.

He demanded harshly, 'What is it?'

'Not quite a cramp.' With bent head she concentrated on her inner self, only straightening when the small twinge faded into nothingness. 'It's gone,' she said on a slow sigh of relief.

Emotion clamped Keir's features, compressed his mouth into a straight line, blazed fiercely as hidden diamonds in his eyes. 'I'll get a doctor.'

Hope shook her head. 'It's probably nothing—just another supercharged hormone acting up.'

Unexpectedly, jerkily, he pulled her into his warm, strong body, holding her against him. 'Everything will be all right,' he promised uncompromisingly, as though by saying it he could make it so.

When he picked her up she exclaimed, 'What are you doing?'

'Taking you to bed.' Her heart jumped, only to lag back to its usual rhythm when he went on, 'Maria will bring up your dinner.'

In spite of her protests he carried her over to the bed and sat her on the side, leaning over to haul back the covers.

'Keir, I think you're overreacting,' she said, a trace of anger curling through her words.

'I won't ring the doctor if you go to bed and stay there until tomorrow morning.'

'You're trying to manipulate me!'

He shrugged, but didn't back down an inch. 'I carry through on my threats. Think of the child.'

Hope narrowed her eyes. Bitterness corroded her voice. 'I hate emotional blackmailers.'

He held her gaze for some moments before bending towards her. Hope's eyelids fluttered down as his mouth touched hers gently, sweetly. 'And this?' he asked, his voice deep and raw. 'Do you hate it when I do this?'

Her voice faded, emerged drowning in hunger and need and love. 'Don't,' she managed at last.

And then the kiss was transformed, losing gentleness, losing sweetness; Keir's mouth plundered her willing one, and she gasped, offering him much more than a simple kiss.

He took his chance and she went up in flames. Desire twisted through her, clouding her mind with its potent witchery, persuading surrender. But she knew enough now to realise that the siren summons wasn't enough. 'No, Keir,' she said against his ardent mouth, her voice husky and laboured. 'It just—complicates things.'

He lifted his head; the crystalline eyes cooled, froze. A wolfish smile hardened his sensual mouth. 'But this is so simple,' he said even as his arms loosened and he stepped back.

'For you,' she said sadly, and gasped, stiffening as another cramp spread across her stomach. She didn't say anything, but she heard Keir swear beneath his breath, then yell for Maria.

Torn by a bitter anguish, she said raggedly, 'Perhaps we should have waited three months before making any decisions—aren't pregnancies more likely to carry to term after that?'

His eyes went opaque, the iron angularity of his bone structure showing starkly through his skin as he said between his teeth, 'I don't ever want to hear you say anything like that again.' His head swivelled as the housekeeper appeared at the door. In a voice Hope had never heard before he ordered, 'Maria, get the helicopter here and ring the doctor.'

CHAPTER ELEVEN

AN HOUR later Hope was lying in a private clinic in Auckland. She'd been processed, examined by the obstetrician she and Keir had seen previously, told that the cramps were almost certainly a mere glitch in the grand scheme of pregnancy, and put to bed.

Stiff with a corrosive fear, she stared at the ceiling and waited for another pang, bitterly aware of the unformed dreams that had lurked just beyond the border of consciousness. Barely formed the baby might be, but if she lost it she'd grieve with all her heart.

And at the back of her mind skulked the furtive, despicable knowledge that if the baby died she'd lose Keir, too.

Perhaps it served her right that she should feel the first cramp just after she'd told him that she couldn't trust him. Even as the thought formulated in her mind her stomach muscles tightened—not yet pain, but ominously threatening.

Breathing slowly and steadily, to a formula, she summoned calming thoughts, determined to give their child the best chance it could have.

The door clicked open, swung closed behind Keir's tall figure. 'How are you?' he asked, coming over to stand by the bed.

Hope kept her eyes on the ceiling. 'I'm fine,' she told him dully, snatching her hand away from her waist.

Sitting down, he enclosed her fingers in his warm ones. 'Try not to worry. You heard what the specialist said—it's almost certainly nothing.'

His warmth went through her like the promise of life.

'If I—if it—if I lose the baby—' her mouth trembled '—I'll go back to Australia.'

'Why?' he asked, that note of harshness more pronounced. Deliberately he went on, 'Because your revenge will have backfired?'

Shocked, she turned her head. The light glowed lovingly on his face, slid in slabs of radiance over high, proud cheek-bones, the blade of his nose and the arrogant thrust of jaw. Framed by dark brows and lashes, his eyes burned like ice under moonlight.

Stumbling, her voice thick, she muttered, 'I don't want any sort of revenge. I never did. You said I was screwed up because of my stepfather—and I think you're right.'

He dropped a kiss on her hand and stood up. 'You're not screwed up. We'll talk when we're back home. Relax now, and go to sleep.'

Watching him move away, she stifled the weakness that almost persuaded her to call out, plead with him not to leave her in this strange place, in this strange bed, alone and lonely...

Disgusted by her need, her dependence, she asked brightly, 'Where are you going?'

He was a dark silhouette filling the doorway. 'I have to ring someone. I'll be back in five minutes or so.'

'You can't stay here.'

'Of course I can.' His voice was calm, completely confident.

She moved uneasily. 'Keir, I'll be all right. You need a decent sleep. Go to your apartment—it's not far from here, is it?'

He paused, then said in a level voice, 'No. Try to trust me, Hope,' and closed the door behind him.

She lay still, monitoring every twinge of muscle, every heartbeat. Resembling a luxurious hotel bedroom, the room itself didn't so much as hint at a hospital, but through the glass panel in the door the corridor light shone with white, cold luminescence.

Was that Keir's voice in the distance? Perhaps he was speaking to the nurse at the station. She strained her ears, but heard only the whine—muted, impersonal—of some machine somewhere, and the occasional hum of traffic outside the windows.

Tears stung her eyes. She shivered, locked by anger and dismay into a hideous stasis as she wondered what she'd do if she lost the baby. Roam an empty world, always lonely...

Perhaps dwelling on the fear might make it happen. Desperately she pushed everything from her brain, and eventually kind sleep and the light sedative they'd given her dragged her beneath the level of consciousness.

When she woke again it was getting light and for a moment she didn't know where she was. Frowning, she looked around, then stiffened as she became aware of another presence in the room. Keir was sitting on the edge of another bed that had been pushed against the wall while she slept. He hadn't noticed that she was awake because he was leaning forward, elbows on knees, head in his hands in an attitude of such despair that she whispered his name.

He looked up sharply, then sprang to his feet and strode rapidly across to her. 'What is it?' he demanded, his voice raw and taut.

Hope couldn't get her brain to work; she croaked lethargically, 'Nothing. I'm thirsty.'

He poured a glass of water, then sat on the bed and eased her up into his arms, holding her against his chest as he held the glass to her lips.

Cold hard practicality warned Hope to shut down her senses so that she couldn't feel his warmth, but the lure of his effortless masculine support kept her still as she sipped gratefully.

'That was lovely,' she said when the glass was empty.

Why had he been sitting like that, as though all he'd ever wanted had abandoned him to emptiness?

He set the glass down on the bedside table. 'Are you all right?'

'Yes,' she said, allowing herself a cautious hope. 'No cramps since last night, unless I've been having them in my sleep.'

'If you have, they've been very mild ones. You haven't moved or made a noise.'

'Have you slept at all?'

'No,' he said, and was silent, still holding her against his chest, one arm supporting her back so that his hand rested beneath her breasts.

She should pull away, but she couldn't. Just this once, she pleaded with some unknown, cruel fate—just let me stay like this, free from the flashfire of passion, enveloped in tenderness.

Above her head he said roughly, 'I'm sorry you found out about Aline like that. And even sorrier that I lost my temper when you taxed me with it. I'd give anything to take back what I did—and what I said.'

Hope twisted so she could see up into his face, all angles and planes, the strong bone structure providing compelling toughness. His mouth was a thin line, the polished silver eyes screened by thick lashes. 'Don't blame yourself,' she said quickly. 'Truly, it wasn't your fault.'

He didn't speak for a few charged seconds, long enough to make her tense and wish that she hadn't told him the truth. Then, still in that level, emotionless voice, he said, 'After you left New Zealand I kept in touch with your mother. Occasionally she'd read something out of one of your letters. Then she died, and I didn't know where the hell you were, or whether I'd ever see you again. Aline came one night—I wish to God it had never happened.'

'Keir,' she whispered, 'it's all right.'

As though she hadn't spoken he said, 'I want this baby desperately because it's yours, nurtured in your body, part of you. And because if you can't learn to trust me it will be the only child I'll have.'

Astonished, her heart bumping noisily in her chest, she twisted to look at him. His features were a stark testimony to force and power, his eyes shards of dazzling ice, ice darkened by the long polar night.

'Why?' she breathed, searching his face for some indication of his meaning.

The muscles in his body coiled and flexed as he moved against the pillows, but his arm didn't tighten around her. She could pull free any time she liked…

Speaking steadily he went on, 'If we lose the baby, don't go back to Australia. Stay here.'

'Keir—'

She was cut off by the abrupt opening of the door and the entrance of a nurse, bright and cheerful and romantic, if the smile she gave them both was any indication. Hope could have killed her.

'I just need to do a couple of things for Ms Sanderson,' the nurse announced, making it more than obvious that she expected Keir to leave.

'A couple of things' meant a shower and a change of clothes, then another check by the obstetrics specialist again, who finally said with a warm smile, 'Relax! As far as I can tell, everything's going to be all right. Now, here comes your breakfast. Eat it up, and then I'll see you and Mr Carmichael together.'

Hugely relieved, Hope settled back, but Keir's last words drummed through her brain, driving away her usually excellent appetite. Glowering at the white gardenia on the tray, she forced down a piece of toast and marmalade and a glass of freshly squeezed orange juice before sitting back against the pillows.

If only the nurse had waited for five more minutes, she thought, torn by a desperate anticipation.

Keir returned as she drained the last of her cup of tea, all prowling, lean-hipped male in casual trousers and a cotton shirt that emphasised his height and the width of his shoulders.

'Oh, wow, what a babe!' a young nurse collecting the tray growled beneath her breath. 'You lucky, lucky thing!' Grinning at them both, she carried the breakfast things out to the trolley.

Keir bent to kiss Hope, a real kiss that choked off her greeting. Flushed, bemused, she stared at him when he smiled, pale eyes gleaming, and said, 'I've just been talking to the obstetrician; you'll almost certainly be able to go home.'

It was too much; Hope tried so hard to stem her tears that her teeth chattered, only to give way completely when she felt Keir's arms come around her. He let her weep for a few minutes, then said quietly, 'The baby's fine, and so are you. I thought she'd told you?'

Eventually she pulled away, muttering, 'Yes, she did. I'm sorry.'

He took out a handkerchief and began to wipe her eyes carefully. Things would be much simpler, Hope thought desperately, if he weren't so thoughtful, so attentive—so bloody brotherly. It was incredibly comforting—and even more depressing. Oh, she wanted his consideration, but she wanted much more than that from this man.

She'd been so careful to avoid any emotional entanglement, yet she'd been ambushed by love.

The obstetrician was even more positive. 'Sometimes in the first three months there's a slight tendency to spot and cramp at the time when periods would have arrived,' she said. 'From the dates you've given me, this is what's happening. So far there's absolutely no sign that you're miscarrying. Rest for a week or so, and no sex until I've given you the all-clear.' She looked meaningly from Hope's hot face to Keir's impassive features, then went on briskly, 'There is absolutely no reason why you shouldn't carry this baby full-term.'

Feeling foolish, Hope said, 'I panicked a bit when I felt the cramps.'

'That's understandable. Try not to worry—pregnancy and birth are entirely natural processes, and a calm mind is very helpful.'

Which was all very well, Hope thought later as she watched the green hills and valleys of Northland unfold through the window of the car. She'd like to be calm, but it was difficult when the man next to her only had to look at her to set the blood spinning through her veins, chasing away common sense and prudence and self-control.

Being with Keir was changing her, altering some essential part of her, and she was afraid. The independence that had always been so precious to her had slipped beyond her reach. Keeping her eyes on the shadowy islands marking the silver-blue sea, she wailed in silent desperation, What's going to happen now?

Keir reached out and took her hand, holding it loosely. Biting her lip, she felt a hidden softening inside her, a slow, irresistible tide of heat and desire and—more dangerous by far—the aching, desperate love that threatened her autonomy.

'What are we going to do about Aline?' she blurted.

His mouth compressed. 'You are going to do nothing,' he said, the hard note in his voice a subtle warning. 'Leave her to me.'

Hope shook her head. 'Keir, don't be hard on her. You were right, she doesn't love you, but I think she's built an awful lot of hopes on you. And this scare had nothing to do with her—her timing was wrong, that's all.'

He gave her a narrow-eyed glance, then lifted her hand

and kissed it. 'You're very kind,' he said against her skin. 'It's all right, I won't be cruel to her. But she's interfered enough; it's time she put her house in order and got on with her life.'

Hope looked at him and nodded, dimly aware that she had arrived at a momentous changing point. Four years previously he'd been a rising star on the Pacific Rim business scene, combining an ice-cold brain, lethal energy—and an almost superhuman instinct for the killing deal—in a relentless drive towards success. Now he'd reached it, and was going further, but nothing would change the man who had taken on the world on his own.

The difference was in her. She trusted him, she thought with astonishment, not to crucify Aline.

'You're right,' she said, and yawned.

'What the hell do you think you're doing?'

Hope glowered at Keir. Speaking slowly and distinctly, she said, 'I am ironing my clothes.'

'Maria—'

'Has her own work to do.' Hope pressed the iron into a cuff, concentrating on making the pleat crisp and neat. 'Keir, I am perfectly well. I haven't had another cramp since the one just before we arrived at the clinic, and that was a week ago. The doctor is very happy with my progress.' She'd even said they could resume marital relations again.

If it hadn't hurt so much Hope would have laughed in the woman's face. Since they'd come home from the clinic Keir had been friendly and considerate, a fascinating, interesting companion, and he hadn't come near her.

Obviously she'd put far too much emphasis on that enigmatic remark *Don't go back to Australia*. It had meant nothing.

She picked up the ironed shirt and slid it carefully onto a hanger.

'I presume,' Keir said, watching her, 'that you still have a rooted objection to getting married before the baby arrives?'

'Yes,' she snapped. Strange how so much could change in a short time. Now she'd bargain her soul away for a chance to win his love.

'Why?'

Goaded, she hung the coathanger up in the cupboard. 'There's a possibility that I might lose the baby. Why bother with a wedding—?'

'I said that I didn't ever want to hear anything like that again.'

The flat, lethal note in his voice should have warned her but she persisted, 'Keir, it's silly to—'

'I know you don't want to marry me,' he said silkily, 'but just think of it as an ongoing revenge.'

Suddenly exhausted by the war she'd been fighting with herself, she turned and faced him. 'Damn you,' she whispered. 'I did not sleep with you to be revenged on you. And, if you must know, I didn't sleep with you because I wanted to get you out of my system, either.' She leaned over and switched the iron off at the wall. The homestead had a huge laundry, clean and well painted, but the years of washing and ironing had left it with a faint, musty, old soap smell.

'Then why?' he asked, pale eyes glinting as he watched her, his angular face cold and hard.

'Because I never stopped loving you,' she spat. She took a step towards him, her fists clenching at her sides, and jerked her chin up to flick damp strands of hair off her face. 'Pathetic, isn't it? I spent four years obsessing about you, so hung up on you that I couldn't fall in love with anyone else, and I didn't even know why!'

His laughter was low and savage, as scornful as the twist of his mouth. 'You don't know what love is. You've cuddled and nurtured your grievance to your heart for four years, and when you saw me again you couldn't wait to unload it, make me pay for something that never happened.'

'I heard—'

'You heard half a conversation! For the last time, Hope, I did not make a deal with your father.'

Her anguished eyes searched his face, met nothing but a cold pride. She said in a voice from which all expression had been banished, 'How can I believe you?'

In a voice as cold as his face he said, 'I can't prove it. You'll have to trust me.'

She closed her eyes. Instinct buzzed wordlessly inside her, warning her, chiding her.

Keir said grimly, 'Is it so difficult to take that final step? You say you love me—if love isn't based on trust, then what is it worth?'

Her eyes flew open as he came across the room. He didn't touch her, but she flinched at the violence of his emotions, the ferocious will-power that barely caged them.

As though she'd hit him, he stopped just out of arm's reach.

'How long do I have to keep proving myself?' he asked in a low, raw voice. He didn't wait for an answer, but muttered in words stripped of everything but a stark, violent need, 'I loved you four years ago, even though it was impossible because you were so young. I loved you when I saw you in that shop in Noosa, when we made love on that bloody uncomfortable bed underneath your landlady's room—I loved you when you told me that you'd only slept with me to get me out of your system.'

'I thought that—but I was wrong,' she said steadily.

He closed his eyes. When he opened them they were burning. 'I love you now,' he said. 'You carry my heart in your hand. That's what love is for me—not just passion, or flirtation, or companionship. Or even this driving, compulsive need. It's a combination of them all, and something extra that is yours alone, and only yours. Hope, I will give you anything you want, agree to anything—you can even live in another house if you want to. I don't want to cage you, take your freedom away. I'm not like James Sanderson. But I need to have you close so that I can prove it to you. I don't care how long it takes, but don't run away again.'

Although shock held her silent, he must have read her incredulous joy—her overwhelming, heart-shaking relief—in her eyes, because his mouth curved dangerously, and he rasped, 'You little witch. Why didn't you tell me?'

But he gave her no time to answer; his head came down and they kissed, a deep kiss of commitment, piercingly satisfying as they allowed the passion they'd kept under such restraint its full freedom.

Keir yawned, and kissed the top of her head.

'Mmf,' Hope groaned, stretching, welcoming the erotic slide of skin against skin, the heat and the flash—followed by the slow burn—of renewed desire. 'Satisfied now that I love you?'

His voice was lazy, richly textured with a love he no longer tried to hide. 'I won't ever be satisfied. You're like a drug I can't get enough of.'

She looked up into molten eyes. 'You know, I was incredibly blind. I can't believe how blind I was! I was so sure I couldn't get you out of my system because we hadn't actually made love. I was positive that if we had an affair I'd get rid of such an inconvenient passion.'

'I really object to being thought of as some sort of disease you can immunise yourself against.' But he was smiling, his gaze tender.

Sighing, Hope rubbed her toes up the inside of his leg, enjoying the way his calf muscles flexed. 'I should have known I'd never be able to vaccinate myself against you. As it was, making love with you really drove me over the edge, but I still wouldn't admit that I loved you.'

'I don't blame you,' he said judicially. 'You overheard a pretty damning conversation.'

'Yet you didn't behave like the demon I'd believed in all these years—and I must have known, deep down, that you weren't, because I wouldn't have trusted you with a place in the baby's life if I'd believed that.'

'I hope not,' he said grimly, 'but I was under no illusions. I'd put you in a hell of a position—pregnant, with no money, no job, no prospects.'

She responded to the fleeting note of self-contempt in his voice with a vigour that startled her. Kissing his shoulder, she muttered, 'I'd have managed.'

'I know,' he said, sounding surprised. His chest lifted in wry laughter. 'I'm learning not to think of you as that unsure eighteen-year-old I fell in love with. When I arrived back in Noosa to find you gone—I knew then that I'd never get over you. If you wanted revenge for the way I dealt with your father's offer four years ago, Hope, you had it then. I damned near tore the place apart, only to find that no one had heard from you—even the Petries had no idea where you were. I made them promise to contact me the minute they heard— and wondered how the hell I was going to find you if you didn't write to them.'

His voice broke; he tilted her face and kissed her with unleashed male power.

'I'm sorry,' she whispered, touching his face lovingly.

'It served me right. Until I got to the Gold Coast and actually saw you I had nightmares, where I searched for you, knowing in that bloody awful way you do in nightmares that you were desperate and lost and calling for me.'

Hope hugged him tightly and kissed him. 'I won't ever run away again.'

'Good.' His smile was tinged with irony. 'Your mother

was right—you needed to get away. But even at eighteen you were strong enough to stand and face anyone. It's one of the reasons I fell in love with you—amongst others,' he murmured, and began to tell her what those other reasons had been, his voice sinking and the faint raw note in it intensifying.

Hope gave up trying to clear the sensual fumes from her head. 'I do love you,' she said, and shivered.

'What's the matter?'

'I wonder whether I'd have gone through life waiting for you if you hadn't happened to arrive in Noosa.'

'I didn't *happen* to arrive,' he said calmly. 'I knew you were there.'

Her head jerked up, catching him on the chin. 'Sorry,' she said, and kissed him there, but lifted her face immediately and scanned his, seeing the truth in his eyes. 'How?' she breathed.

'Just after...' He paused, then said deliberately, 'After Aline and I made love, I got a letter from your mother's lawyer. She'd asked him to send me your address a year after her death.'

'When I left home I promised her I'd tell the solicitor whenever I changed my address,' Hope murmured, tears stinging behind her eyes. 'Every so often she reminded me of that, and asked me to keep on notifying him no matter what happened. I thought she just wanted someone to know where I was, but I'm so glad I did it.'

'So am I.' He kissed the place where her hair swept back from her brow, his mouth lingering. 'I organised the meeting with the Chinese delegation and came over. I told myself I needed to be sure that you were all right.'

Hope didn't know that she liked this.

He said wryly, 'I lied, of course. You'd haunted me ever since you left New Zealand. I had to find out what sort of woman you'd become; at twenty-three you were old enough to make some decisions about your life.'

He had let her go to find her own freedom. She couldn't imagine James Sanderson setting anyone free to find her own life. In him the lust for power had burned too fiercely.

Keir might be a dominant man, but not a dominating one.

'But when I got there you looked at me as though you didn't recognise me. It was like being kicked in the heart.' His kiss was almost a punishment. When it was over, he murmured against her lips, 'I stood in the door of that jeweller's shop and I wanted you so much I could feel the hunger clawing through every cell in my body. I felt damn near bent double with it. I knew then that I wasn't going to be able to turn my back and leave you, so I used everything I could to persuade you to go out with me, to get used to me again. And then you threw me by telling me what sort of man your stepfather was, and I realised that it wasn't going to be simple to gain your trust. Making love to you wasn't going to be enough, even though you blew my mind with your passionate response.'

'I'm surprised you persevered,' she said wryly, running an exploratory finger down his spine.

'I was in too deep by then to think of giving up. But I swear I didn't plan on getting you pregnant.'

He stroked across her newly sensitive breasts, cupping them, his long fingers darkly dramatic against her pale, satiny skin.

'Of course you didn't!' She sighed and snuggled closer, then sat up abruptly and glared at him. 'Why did you wait so long to tell me this? It's been a week since I came home from the clinic!'

His smile was self-derisory. 'I wanted you well and strong enough to hear it.' And then he laughed beneath his breath. 'The truth is that I was afraid to push my luck. Materially I can give you everything you want; you'd even admitted to loving me—but you still didn't trust me.'

She gave him a quick glance, and said sombrely, 'It is so—huge a thing, to be dependent on someone else for your happiness.'

'As long as it's a two-way process, does it matter so much?' His eyes kindling with naked need, he held her hand over his heart. 'I'm scared, too, Hope, because I love you more than I can even admit to myself. With you I'm vulnerable. You have the power to hurt me beyond anything I've ever endured.'

He did understand. Keeping her eyes fixed on his, she nodded.

'So I tried to show you that you could have your independence as well as my love, that real love doesn't involve capitulation.'

Beneath her palm she felt the slow driving beat of his heart. A swift flare of emotion held her silent, until she smiled and with tear-filled eyes said shakily, 'So, we'll be scared together.'

His smile was tender. 'You're a lot stronger than you think. You wouldn't let anyone terrorise you.'

'No,' she said quietly. 'I thought loving a man meant giving up everything that made you a woman—giving up your pride and your independence and your right to any freedom, even of the mind. That's why I didn't want to love anyone, ever.'

Stone-faced, he said, 'I wasn't ever going to tell you this, but I think you need to know. Your mother told me that James Sanderson threatened to take you away from her if she left him. She suspected that that's why he adopted you—it gave him legal leverage over her. She might have loved him to begin with, Hope, but she stayed because of you.'

Hope went white. 'I see. Yes, of course,' she said numbly.

Keir's arms tightened around her. She relaxed into the warmth and strength of his body, before lifting her head. 'I don't approve of revenge,' she said between her teeth, 'but it strikes me as entirely suitable that he should be unable to control anything in his life now.'

'You don't have to worry about him ever again.'

A shiver scudded the length of her spine. 'I'm not afraid of him; I just don't want anything to do with him. And if that seems terrible—well, I'm terrible.'

'Why should you want anything to do with him? He might have adopted you, but he was no father,' Keir said brutally. 'He can't hurt you any more. Did your birth father have any relatives?'

'I don't think so,' she said blankly.

'Would you like to look?' Keir asked. 'I don't have many, and you don't have any on your mother's side, so our baby will need all the relatives it can get.' He bent and kissed her waist, letting his mouth linger over the spot where the obstetrician said the baby lay.

Fire smouldered through her as he said, 'We won't be perfect parents, Hope, and I won't be a perfect husband, but I'll love you until I die, and we'll do our best for this baby and any others we might have. That's all we can do—love them and let them be their own person, then let them go when they're ready.'

The shadow of loneliness that had haunted her all her life lifted, leaving her in the sunlight of Keir's love. Together they'd create a safe haven for their children, and for each other.

'I love you so much,' she said, like a vow.

He lifted his dark head and smiled at her, the barriers down, his ice-coloured eyes completely transparent to her at last. 'And I love you,' he said. 'We'll make it, my dearest heart.'

* * *

Three weeks later they were married in the garden; the sun shone on green lawns and bright flowers and the creamy froth of clematis over an arbour. The roses hadn't progressed beyond budhood, but those Hope carried were almost open—golden as the diamond around her neck, glowing against her hair and skin like the promise of fulfilment.

Ten people stood around them: Keir's best friend Leo Dacre and his composer wife Tansy, with their two small boys, a middle-aged cousin of Keir's with her husband, and the four Petries.

A year later, when small Emma Jane Carmichael gazed around with eyes that were going to be the exact colour of her mother's—or so her adoring father insisted—the same ten people joined a much larger crowd on the lawn, this time for a christening party. It was a joyous occasion, noisy and fun, with small children squabbling to hold the baby and eat the cake, and Emma dealing with being passed from lap to welcoming lap with a confidence that was, her mother said, inherited from her father.

When it was over, the house quiet and the baby sleeping peacefully, Keir bent to kiss his wife. 'All right?'

'I thought we made a deal about questions like that.' She returned his kiss with slow sensuousness. 'But if you break it, so can I. Thank you,' she whispered.

'Why?'

She pushed a lock of dark hair back from his brow. His eyes gleamed with the special glint that told her he was aroused. 'For being you,' she said. 'For loving me. For bringing me to life.'

He laughed beneath his breath and looked so deeply into her eyes she thought he saw her soul. 'How can I not love you? You're everything I need, all that I want, the sum and substance of my life. I thought I couldn't be happier when I discovered that you loved me, but now that Emma's here I know that love expands into infinity. I thank you for that.'

As Hope reached up to kiss his beautiful mouth again his arms closed around her, and her last thought before the honeyed tide of oblivion overtook them both was that this was her life—Keir, their child, their friends, all linked in the charmed circle of their love.

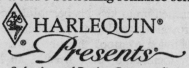

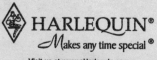

COOPER'S CORNER

In April 2002 you are invited to three wonderful weddings in a very special town...

A Wedding at Cooper's Corner

USA Today bestselling author

Kristine Rolofson
Muriel Jensen
Bobby Hutchinson

Ailing Warren Cooper has asked private investigator David Solomon to deliver three precious envelopes to each of his grandchildren. Inside each is something that will bring surprise, betrayal...and unexpected romance!

And look for the exciting launch of *Cooper's Corner,* a NEW 12-book continuity from Harlequin— launching in August 2002.

The world's bestselling romance series.

HARLEQUIN®
Presents

Seduction and Passion Guaranteed!

GREEK TYCOONS

They're the men who have everything—except a bride...

Wealth, power, charm—what else could a heart-stoppingly handsome tycoon need? In the GREEK TYCOONS miniseries you have already been introduced to some gorgeous Greek multimillionaires who are in need of wives.

Now it's the turn of favorite Presents author

Helen Brooks,

with her attention-grabbing romance

THE GREEK TYCOON'S BRIDE

Harlequin Presents #2255
Available in June

This tycoon has met his match, and he's decided he *has* to have her...*whatever* that takes!

Pick up a Harlequin Presents® novel and you will enter a world of spine-tingling passion and provocative, tantalizing romance!

Available wherever Harlequin books are sold.

HARLEQUIN®
Makes any time special ®